R.W. WALLACE

Author of the Tolosa Mystery Series

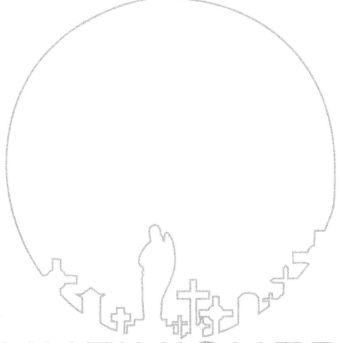

UNFINISHED BUSINESS

A Ghost Detective Collection

VOLUME 2

Unfinished Business
Volume 2
by R.W. Wallace

"Family History" Copyright © 2021 by R.W. Wallace
"Heritage" Copyright © 2021 by R.W. Wallace
"New Beginnings" Copyright © 2022 by R.W. Wallace
"Far From Home" Copyright © 2022 by R.W. Wallace
"Severed Ties" Copyright © 2021 by R.W. Wallace

Cover by R.W. Wallace
Cover Illustration 10926765 © germanjames | 123rf.com
Cover Illustration 82772248 © zwiebackesser | Depositphotos
Cover Illustration 263199440 © Nouman | Adobe Stock

All characters and events in this book, other than those clearly in the public domain, are fictitious and any resemblance to real persons, living or dead, is purely coincidental.

All rights reserved. No part of this publication may be reproduced, distributed, or transmitted in any form or by any means, including photocopying, recording, or other electronic or mechanical methods, without the prior written permission of the publisher, except in the case of brief quotations embodied in critical reviews and certain other noncommercial uses permitted by copyright law.

www.rwwallace.com
Varden Publishing
Unit 95090, PO Box 6945, London, W1A 6US

ISBN paperback: [978-2-493670-16-8]
ISBN ebook: [978-2-493670-17-5]

TABLE OF CONTENTS

INTRODUCTION

THE GHOST DETECTIVE series came to life while I was doing a short story challenge in 2018. I can't even remember why I started writing about these ghosts screaming their heads off as their caskets were lowered into the ground, I just know the characters immediately felt like good friends, and that I wanted to see what else they might get up to.

So I kept writing the shorts, one ghost with unfinished business at the time. Some were pure mysteries, some tended more toward "finding peace with yourself." I loved writing all of them.

All the stories in this volume have first been published in *Pulphouse Fiction Magazine*. The editor, Dean Wesley Smith, does me the honor of buying every single Ghost Detective story I send him, and I'm always thrilled to see my stories in such good company.

Of course, there was also that one short story that was supposed to showcase Robert and Clothilde's own unfinished business. It didn't take me many pages to realize that was *not* a short story. Halfway through the novel, I realized it wasn't even just a single book, but a series.

So if you're interested in the main character's search for justice, check out the novel *Beyond the Grave*. At the time of writing this note, I'm in the process of writing the fifth book in the series.

And I'm still having fun with it.

But for now, please enjoy these five Ghost Detective short stories. And feel free to let me know what you think through a review!

R. W. Wallace
www.rwwallace.com

FAMILY HISTORY

A Ghost Detective Short Story

BOOK 6

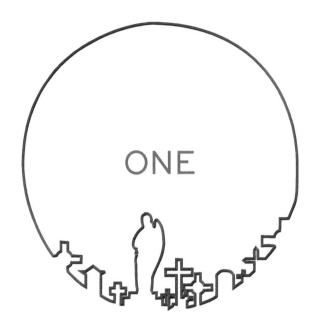

ONE

OUR CEMETERY IS a small one. I haven't actually counted, but there can't be more than three hundred tombs total and at least ninety-five percent of those never became ghosts.

The ones who did have all found their peace and moved on—present company and Clothilde excluded.

The people of our little town don't fall dead like flies or anything, but little by little we're running out of space. Some years ago, the municipality gave us a neighboring lot, but even that's already half-full.

The new section is not as fun to walk around in as the older parts because nobody can afford—or are willing to part with large sums of money for—the huge stone constructions with statues and seatings and columns that were in favor a century ago. Today everybody goes with the classic tombstone, a short inscription, and possibly a plaque with a picture of the deceased. And let's not forget the plastic flowers.

The new tombs in the north section are arranged in neat rows with straight, clean paths, whereas the oldest section to the west has winding paths, overgrown passages, and some graves that have completely disappeared beneath overenthusiastic weeds.

There's no such thing as an eternal resting place, of course—not in a graveyard like this, anyway. It's possible to buy your lot "à perpétuité," for all eternity. Except in the French graveyards, eternity means one hundred years.

Lately, the church or municipality or whoever it is who's responsible for the graveyards have been digging up the old graves where the hundred years are up and there are no descendants to pay to keep the lot, in order to free up space.

In a couple of cases, the descendants were found and decided to keep paying. They even came in and cleaned up the tombstones, making sure there was room for more family members. It certainly makes the place look more pleasant.

In most cases, though, the tombstones are removed, whatever remains still intact are removed, and the lot cleared for new arrivals.

In all honesty, it's a bit disturbing to watch this happen, especially for a pair of ghosts who still haven't moved on and can't help but wonder what will happen to them if they still haven't done so when their time is up.

Watching someone exhume a body isn't particularly fascinating. But it's the only entertainment we have. Whenever a new ghost arrives, we make sure to be ready when they exit their caskets, to explain the ins and outs of being a ghost in this cemetery. Most importantly, we help them figure out what it is they need to move on, what unfinished business we can help them wrap up.

When there are no other ghosts, we watch the excavations.

"Do we know who was in this one?" Clothilde asks me.

We're sitting on the neighboring tombstone—the Lambert family, whose first family member arrived in 1859 and most recent only two years ago; one of those places which always has fresh flowers year round—having watched the excavator remove the tombstone, now giving place to the manual labor of three young men.

I shake my head. "I never managed to read the name. Seems like it's only one person, though, and I'm pretty sure he or she died in nineteen seventeen."

"Municipality certainly isn't losing any time," Clothilde comments dryly.

I don't exactly know why we're sitting here watching, but it just feels right. Paying our last respects to the deceased, maybe. Hoping someone will do it for us when our time comes.

Because, let's face the truth. If we don't get any visitors now, we certainly won't have anyone to pay to keep our space in seventy years.

The men doing the excavation aren't the usual gravediggers. It seems like the municipality isn't working on the same contract as the people responsible for putting people *into* the earth.

7

I don't like these guys as much as the usual team. I don't expect them to stay perfectly serious for hours on end, but the jokes I'm hearing are anything but respectful. These guys are doing the job because it's the only job they could find, and they're not pretending to like it.

"Seriously," one of them says as he throws a shovelful of dirt haphazardly onto the path next to the grave, "I don't see why we have to do this manually at all. Can't they just use the excavator to get everything out? Who cares if they accidentally get part of the idiots from the tomb next door? It's not like anybody'll know."

We'd know.

But we can't tell anybody. My frown mirrors Clothilde's.

The second guy, a weaselly-looking guy with a shaved head and dark, close-set eyes, grunts in agreement. "The dead don't care. If I keel over tomorrow, just throw me in a ditch somewhere."

I open my mouth to say something to Clothilde, but I'm interrupted by a shovel hitting wood. The casket.

"Got 'im," Weasel-face says. "Let's see what state he's in."

During past excavations, they've unearthed caskets and bodies in various states of decomposition. Sometimes the casket is intact and the skeleton laid out prettily inside—possibly with pretty decent clothing. Sometimes the casket has disintegrated completely, and only parts of the skeleton can be removed, the rest having been eaten up by the earth, ending up who knows where.

When they get a whole skeleton, they have to take it to some sort of pauper's grave. For obvious reasons, they can't just throw them in the trash.

The three workers remove the earth, bringing to light a casket that still has the shape and look of a casket, but looks like it could disintegrate any second.

"There's no way that's coming out in one piece," one of the men says.

"I'm not touching any more dead bodies," the second says, his hands raised as if giving up. "We're not paid enough for his shit."

"Maybe we won't have to." Weasel-face steps up right next to the casket, raises his shovel above his head, and brings it down full force on the center of the flimsy wood.

The entire lid cracks under the pressure, and goes from being a large, even surface to a million splinters in two seconds flat.

Weasel-face nods in satisfaction. "I'm thinking this is one of the graves where we didn't find anything."

His colleague lights up with a wicked grin. "Oh, I see. Let me help." He takes his own shovel and hits the side of the casket, with much the same result as earlier.

"I really don't like these guys," I say as I turn to Clothilde. "How come there's no—"

"Robert." Clothilde's voice is shaking and her eyes are wide and non-blinking. You'd think she's seen a ghost, pun intended.

She points to the grave and my gaze follows, puzzled what has her so shook up.

I let out a strangled cry.

There's someone in the casket.

A young man, maybe in his twenties—it's difficult to tell with all the splinters and dirt superposed with his form—is lying in the casket, his arms crossed and an annoyed frown marring his smooth forehead.

A shovel runs right through his abdomen and he winces.

"Well, this is certainly uncomfortable."

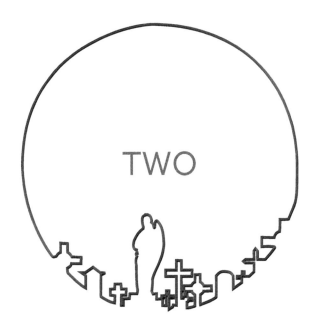

TWO

THERE'S A GHOST in a hundred-year-old grave.

"How long have you been down there?" I ask, dumbfounded.

The three workers are discovering that their method is working and all start hacking at the casket and its contents with more energy than I've ever seen from them. Two out of three hits go right through the ghost and I can see him flinching every time they hit the bones.

I can see he's going to answer my question, but I cut him off. "Please come out of there, that can't be comfortable." I extend a hand—as if he needs it or can indeed grab it—urging him to move.

Reluctantly—I can see the defeated sigh and note how he studies the three men before deciding that they have no intention of stopping anytime soon—he sits up, then quickly jumps to his feet and steps out of the casket.

"Come up here, why don't you?" Clothilde pats the slab of smooth granite next to her. "Let the idiots do their vandalism in peace."

With another sigh, the man complies, though he takes a while to figure out how to get out of the grave. It's a whole new world to get used to when you become a ghost, where you have to decide which part of the physical realm you want to respect, and which one you'll ignore.

Clothilde, for example, has a great love for the *tops* of tombstones—great seats—but has no need for the sides. She always sits the same way; her butt on the top and her feet swinging straight through the granite as if it weren't there.

The man figures it out fairly quickly, all things considered, and is soon sitting—back straight as a ramrod, hair brushed to a perfect early-twentieth-century haircut, straight parting and all, and his suit and bow tie immaculately ironed—next to Clothilde.

"I guess we should start with introductions," I say lamely. "I'm Robert."

"Clothilde." She offers her hand for him to shake, and after a very short hesitation he takes it.

"Bernard Lebrun," he says, his voice cultured.

I have no idea what to say to the man, so I just launch into my usual spiel for when we have new arrivals. "We're the only ghosts currently in residence in this cemetery. If you need any help with moving on, we'd love to help."

He studies me for a second. "Moving on?"

"Yes. Uh…you know. Moving on to wherever ghosts go when they've handled their unfinished business."

"For obvious reasons," Clothilde interjects with a smile, "we don't know where that place is, since we haven't gone there ourselves yet."

"Yet you are more than willing to help me move to this place."

I frown. "I'm one hundred percent sure it's a better place than here. So of course we want to help."

Monsieur Lebrun's presence deeply disturbs me for some reason. How could he just be lying there in his casket without us knowing about it? Has he seriously been there since he died? For over a hundred years? The idea is baffling.

And actually…the most important question might be: Why didn't he come out?

A ghost is kept in place by his or her casket as long as they haven't accepted that they're dead. If the acceptance isn't there, the casket stays a prison. Personally, I spent four days screaming and banging at the walls of my casket before I came to terms with my fate and was let out. Some were quicker, some slower.

But a hundred years?

And what will it mean if he *hasn't* accepted that he's dead? Could he be some sort of danger to us or others? If nothing else, if he's been stuck in a casket for that long, his mind should have broken long ago.

"Why are you so keen on assisting me, if you have not yet obtained this 'moving on' for yourselves? I never had much faith in so-called philanthropists."

All right, his mind seems to be in working order.

Clothilde flashes a huge smile. "We're complicated, is all," she says. "We're kind of limited in our field of action here, so we're waiting patiently for our opening."

I still don't know the details around Clothilde's death, I just know it made quite few waves when she died, and that as a result, nobody ever comes to visit her grave. My friend is as close-mouthed as they get, on top of being stuck for all eternity with the aggressiveness and resistance to authority of a teenager, so I don't push for information.

Some day, she'll tell me.

Monsieur Lebrun glances around the cemetery, taking it in for the first time. "I presume the field of action is the cemetery?"

"You presume correctly!" Clothilde winks at me, her smile still in place.

I can't hold my questions in anymore. "When did you die?"

Monsieur Lebrun's sharp gaze meets mine and holds it for several moments. I'm not sure what he's looking for, but he must have found it, because he answers. "November nineteen seventeen." He takes in my clothing, Clothilde's clothing, the three men continuing their gleeful destruction of his last resting place. "What year is it now?"

"Twenty nineteen," I tell him, watching closely for a reaction. "The reason they're unearthing your grave is that the *perpétuité* is up."

His eyebrows make a minuscule jump. If I hadn't been paying close attention, I might have missed it. This man is very, very good at keeping his feelings to himself.

Clothilde shifts sideways on her seat so she's facing our new arrival. She doesn't even try to hide her curiosity. "You must have had *some* inkling of time passing. You've really been down there all this time?"

Monsieur Lebrun brushes a nonexistent piece of lint off his pants. "Where else would I have been?"

"I don't know." Clothilde raises her hands and shoulders in a way that is very close to, but not quite, mocking. "I'm just curious as to why you wouldn't have come out sooner, is all." She waves a hand between the two of us. "We've both been here for thirty years, and we've never had *any* idea that there was someone in this grave."

"I was perfectly comfortable where I was," Monsieur Lebrun says, his back becoming just a little bit straighter. "I don't see what the point of coming out would be."

Clothilde gapes at him. "So you were happy to just stay down there for all eternity?"

"I was comfortable, as I said. And nobody bothered me. I don't see why I would seek out a place filled with people screaming all the time."

"Ah," I say. "So you heard the screams of the new arrivals, huh?" I cock my head at him. "You never thought to go check?"

He meets my eyes, and I'm not entirely sure if it's indifference I see, or if it's some sort of very strict view of what's proper or not. The man's unreadable. "It was not my place."

"Who cares about 'your place'?" Clothilde says with an eye roll. "You're dead."

"All the more reason to behave in a proper manner."

An awkward silence descends, only interrupted by shovels hitting wood and bones. I can tell when they're hitting poor Bernard Lebrun's skeleton both by the difference in sound and the tiny shudders wracking his body at each hit.

Clothilde chews her lip as she surveys the ongoing massacre. "So what's the proper etiquette for when someone's whacking your casket and dead corpse to pieces?"

Monsieur Lebrun's eyes move to look down into his own grave and I realize he's avoided looking at it ever since he came out.

He gulps. "I don't know."

THREE

"THERE MUST BE *some* sort of unfinished business for you to resolve." Clothilde sits on the edge of the hole that still holds Monsieur Lebrun's remains but looks like a newly dug—and empty—grave. Her ankle-length jeans and worn Converse swing back and forth, into the air, through the dirt, back out in the air.

Monsieur Lebrun leans against the Lamberts' tomb next door, apparently the most relaxed position he's capable of adopting. Not needing to breathe doesn't stop him from sniffing. "I would never leave any business unfinished, Mademoiselle. Once one starts an action, one follows through."

I know Clothilde well enough to know she's laughing on the inside, but luckily she keeps it internal. "And what if one dies while in the midst of an action?"

"That was not the case." Lebrun adjusts his bow tie. "Everything was in order in the shop. It was the first of the month and I'd done the finances and checked the stock. The shop was clean and ready for the month to come."

"You died in nineteen seventeen, right?" I ask.

Lebrun nods. "First of November nineteen seventeen."

"How come you weren't on the front lines? I'm surprised an able-bodied man in his early twenties was still managing his shop in the peaceful part of the country."

Lebrun meets my eyes and it's the first time I see emotion in his eyes. There's some anger, some annoyance…and shame. I'd recognize that look anywhere.

God knows I saw it often enough in the mirror when I was still alive.

"I may not have moved around much since I arrived in this cemetery," Lebrun said in a low but firm voice, "but I've become very well acquainted with how a ghost's 'body' works. It behaves and looks like I expect it to. Mademoiselle here expects the ground to stop her body from falling into the ground, but she does not expect it to resist when she wants to swing her legs." He puts a hand on his right leg. "I now expect my legs to work, so they do. But while I was alive, this was not the case. I suffered an accident from horseback when I was seventeen and had to make do with a bum leg that just barely accepted to hold my weight with the help of a cane. I was not able to participate in the Great War."

And that was his greatest shame. I didn't need for him to elaborate to know that. While I was alive, I'd participated in the November eleventh arrangements in this village several times, and the list of dead was impressively long for such a small place. I'd often wondered if there were even any men left to create the next generation—which would get the honor of dying in the next World War.

At least one man was left behind—but if he'd died before the end of the war, he wouldn't even have been able to help reboost the population.

"How did you die, anyway?" Clothilde's thoughts must have gone in much the same direction as mine.

Lebrun's lips thin as his gaze goes from Clothilde to the open grave to me. "I do not know," he finally says.

"You don't know?" Clothilde meets my eyes. "That's new."

Lebrun's forehead creases slightly into a frown. He's either becoming more expressive or I've just gotten used to him and know how to read him. Right now he's annoyed and defensive.

"I went to sleep on the night of November first and never woke up."

"So…" Clothilde glances between the two of us. "A stroke, perhaps? Heart attack. Choked on a spider in his sleep?"

I hold back my laugh. Barely.

"Do any of those options sound probable to you?" I ask our new friend.

He shifts a little but is still stiff like a stick against the Lamberts' tombstone. "I certainly did not choke on a spider. One never knows for a stroke or a heart attack, but I was in fairly good shape, bum leg notwithstanding, and only twenty-three."

"Maybe that's your unfinished business," Clothilde offers. "To figure out how you died."

I shake my head. "Too weak. I've never met a ghost who just needed to know *how* he died. Catching their killer, sure. Tying up loose ends with friends or family, certainly. But the how is a lot less important than the why."

Clothilde shifts her gaze to Lebrun. "Do you know *why* you died?"

Lebrun just stares back woodenly.

"You're certain there was nobody you needed to say goodbye to?" I ask. "Or tell them you loved them—or anything in that vein?"

Lebrun shakes his head curtly, though I think I might have seen his left eye twitch at the mention of love. Or I might have imagined it. There are statues in this graveyard with more facial expressions than this guy.

I clap my hands briskly. "Then I propose we work on the assumption that you were murdered and that your unfinished business is to at least identify who the killer was."

Clothilde's eyebrows shoot up. "We're going to catch a murderer from nineteen seventeen? Unless it's another undiscovered ghost in this very graveyard, I have no idea how we'd go about that."

I nod. "I'm sure the presumed murderer is dead. But ghosts are all here for a reason. If Monsieur Lebrun's business was impossible to wrap up, I'm sure he would have moved on. There's no point in holding him here for all eternity."

A softness creeps into Clothilde's eyes. "You really believe that?" Her voice is softer than usual and her eyes are searching mine for truth.

"Of course," I tell her. "Our time will come, Clothilde. The world just isn't ready for us yet." I wink at her and get the hoped-for smile in return.

Clothilde's carefree demeanor pops back into place. "So where do we start?"

Lebrun clears his throat, in that way that people like him have, where you clearly understand that they're annoyed at you. "I did not give you authorization to search for anything. You will not be looking into my life and my business. I would have been perfectly happy to stay in my grave forever, and it was in no way my choice to be here in your company."

"Aw, we like hanging out with you, too," Clothilde says.

"You came out of your grave now for a reason," I tell him firmly. "Something will happen that will lead us to your murderer—or whatever else your unfinished business is. Believe me, you do not want to stay in this cemetery forever. Clothilde will make you want to die all over again within a month."

"Hey!"

"We will help you in this, and you will find peace." I might not be able to find it for myself yet, but I've made it my mission to help others get there. In fact, I'm absolutely certain it's part of my own path to redemption.

Lebrun shakes his head, but doesn't say anything, so I take it as approval.

"So what's the plan, boss?" Clothilde asks with a wink.

"The plan?" I look around the cemetery, but everything is as it has always been—dead and barren.

I shrug and lean back on the path behind me, imagining being able to feel the heat of the sunlight on my skin. "We wait."

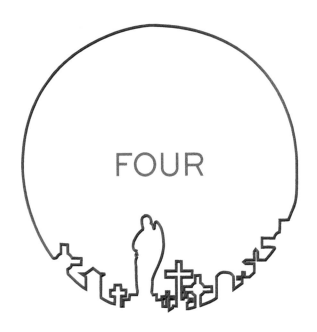

FOUR

ALL IN ALL, we don't have to wait long.

Five days later, the Lamberts come on their monthly visit to refresh the flowers on their tomb. It seems to be some sort of regular Sunday outing for the family, where at least two family members will come on foot, stroll through the cemetery, and spend some time at their lot.

I find it admirable that they're all so dedicated to maintaining the last resting place of their dead ancestors, but also find it a little bit weird. No other family is this regular and they aren't even particularly religious.

Sometimes it's just two adults; sometimes it's entire families, with kids of all ages, from newborn to sullen teenager. None of them ever complain. Then again, seeing how they'll bring a picnic when the weather permits, maybe it isn't all that surprising. If you're not bothered by the fact that it's a graveyard, it's just a calm spot and a nice opportunity to catch up with the family gossip.

At least once a month, we hear the story of how this tradition started—how Mamie's mother came here every week without fail, to give thanks to her husband for coming home long enough to give her her family. If it weren't for that short month, none of them would have even existed.

Today, it's a small procession, but it encompasses no less than four generations of Lamberts, all women. The youngest is no older than a year and is the reason it takes the group forever to cross the cemetery. She wants to walk by herself, but isn't particularly stable on her feet and gets distracted by the real flowers, the fake flowers, the shiny lettering on the gravestones, and the pebbles on the road. When her mother gets impatient and picks her up, the poor baby starts screaming her heart out and is quickly put back down.

The mother is a beautiful young woman in her mid-twenties. She has long, golden hair, dark brown eyes, and a slightly upturned nose. Her own mother walks next to her, with the same brown eyes and the same nose, but with darker and shorter hair. I'd say she's approaching sixty.

The group's eldest member is Geraldine Lambert, known by everyone as Mamie Lambert, and she's eighty if she is a day. She's been a regular here since way before my arrival thirty years ago. She loves walking, so no matter what the weather's like, she'll show up on foot. Possibly with a raincoat and boots, with her pants splattered in water and mud, but she'll be there.

The first time I saw her, she could already qualify as an elderly woman, but she carries herself with such grace, it feels wrong to comment on the deepening lines of her face or the sagging skin at her neck. Her class and inner calm shine through everything, and there's no doubt the young men must have been standing in line to court her in her youth. Her hair is now all white, but I know it used to be blond like her granddaughter's, and her eyes are still a soft, calming brown. And she has the Lambert nose, of course.

The reason why this is still a Lambert grave, and not a Vanderwalle one, is one of the family's favorite stories during these outings. Mamie married young, before she even turned eighteen. She had the time to pop out one daughter and get pregnant with a second one before becoming a widow. Considering two years of marriage wasn't reason enough to go through life with a name she could hardly spell herself, let alone anyone else, she changed it back to Lambert and renamed her children while she was at it.

Mamie Lambert's daughter, Sylvie Lambert—she was a Bertrand for fifteen years, but took her maiden name back after the divorce—carries a bag, which I'm sure contains fresh flowers. Her sister sometimes try to put up fake flowers, claiming it'll save them all money, but Sylvie will have none of it. She'll remove anything plastic whenever she comes, and replace it with the real stuff. Today, we're getting some purple flower that I don't know the name of.

While Sylvie takes care of the flowers, the three others approach the freshly dug hole in the lot next to theirs.

"What happened here?" Mamie asks.

"Probably nobody wanted to pay once the *perpétuité* was up," Sylvie says as she arranges the flower's leaves just so. "Remember they contacted us almost a year ago and we had to pay to keep our place?"

Mamie's wrinkles deepen as her face folds into a frown. "That. Wanting to kick us out of our cemetery."

"They didn't want to kick us out, Mamie," Sylvie says soothingly as she brushes her hands on her pants. "The time that Grand-Mamie paid for was up, is all. Now we're good for another hundred years of Lamberts."

Mamie grunts but lets the subject go.

Us three ghosts are standing on the other side of the open grave, observing the family. Clothilde and I usually come and hang out with the Lamberts when they visit because they're so lively and gay, unlike most of out visitors. For Lebrun, this is his first visit ever and I'm not quite sure how he feels about it.

While the three women study Lebrun's final resting place—or what's left of it—Lebrun goes over to study *their* tomb.

He runs a finger over the large "Lambert" engraved in the arch on top. A shiver runs through him as he realizes his fingers aren't giving him any additional information and he puts his hand behind his back instead.

His eyes move over to the names of the family members interred here. There are over a dozen, but his gaze seems to lock onto the first one and stop there.

I know the names by heart, not only because I've lived here for thirty years and have gotten *very* bored at times, but also because the Lamberts always tell numerous anecdotes during their picnics, keeping the story of their family alive.

That first name: Pierre-Antoine Lambert. Born the first of September 1895, died the third of March 1918.

"He died during the war?" Lebrun asks me when I step up next to him.

"Technically, yes," I reply. "But he was back from the front by then. Came back injured, and just had enough time to get his wife pregnant before succumbing to a bacteria he probably picked up during his convalescence."

"He came back?" Lebrun's eyes stare directly into mine for the first time. "When?"

I exhale, trying to remember the details. I've heard that story at least a hundred times, though. "His wife received the news just before All Hallow's Eve, and he arrived for Christmas. 'Best Christmas gift a wife could hope for.' Mamie Lambert was born in July 1918—a little early, but in great health nonetheless.

Lebrun stares at the women looking into his own grave, his eyes unfocused.

I'm about to ask him if he knew the original Lambert, but I'm interrupted by a scream.

I catch a glimpse of something pink pitching into Lebrun's grave.

The young mother jumps into the hole.

Sylvie screams, her arms out, trying to hold back her daughter a few seconds too late.

Mamie Lambert leans forward to look into the freshly dug grave. "You should keep a better watch on your offspring, Audrey. She could fall into a grave or something."

FIVE

CLOTHILDE IS LOOKING up at me from the bottom of the grave when I join the commotion. "She's fine," she says, and I can tell from the lack of mischievous glint in her eye that she'd been genuinely scared for the little girl. "She's mostly just scared."

The little girl is screaming her heart out in her mother's arms, large tears streaming down her chubby cheeks. The mother seems to be taking as much comfort in her daughter's arms as she's giving. Her eyes are squeezed shut and she's sitting in the fresh dirt in total disregard of her pastel pink jeans, rocking her daughter and touching her everywhere, searching for wounds.

"I think she's all right," she says, her voice cracking.

"Thank God," Sylvie sighs. "Why weren't you watching her?"

"I was watching her!" Audrey screams. "But you can't watch a kid every second of every day. She wanted to pick a flower from the next grave over and tipped over backward into this nightmare."

I jump down into the grave to join Clothilde behind the mother and child. Lebrun has stayed by the Lambert grave and although I can't be one hundred percent certain, I think his eyes are glued to the name of the original Lambert, the one who died just a month or two after him.

Mamie Lambert takes charge of the situation. With a hand on her daughter's shoulder, she addresses her granddaughter. "Accidents happen with toddlers all the time, there's no way to avoid it. We all do our best, as I know you do, Audrey."

Sylvie visibly takes a deep breath, her eyes closed. "I'm sorry, honey. I shouldn't have yelled at you like that."

"Now." Mamie Lambert looks around the empty graveyard. "How do we get you out of there?"

Getting the little girl out would have been easy—if she'd accept letting go of her mother. While Audrey can reach the top of the grave with her hands, she can't pull herself out, especially with her girl clinging to her like a monkey. There's no real hand-hold or stepping stones and the one time she tries to kick a step into the dirt, part of the wall falls down.

"We're going to have to call for help," Audrey says to the two women watching her from the foot of the grave. "I can't risk bringing the walls down on the both of us."

Audrey sits back down in the dirt with her back against a

wall. Clothilde and I sit down next to her. She might not know we're there, but people can sometimes subconsciously realize we're there or even integrate some things we say to them.

The little girl has stopped crying and is currently pulling on her mother's hair, shoving it into the dirt. The fact that Audrey doesn't even seem to mind shows how wiped out she is.

Sylvia is on the phone with someone, explaining the situation, when the little girl lets out a happy gurgle. She holds something in her chubby little hand and holds it up in front of her mother's face.

"What have you got there, honey?" Audrey says. "Is it a rock?" She takes the object from her daughter in order to hold it farther away from her eyes.

"Uh," Clothilde whispers. "I think that's a bone."

I lean in to study it. "Oh, yeah. That's a human bone. Maybe something from the hand? Or the foot?" I glance up at Lebrun, who's flexing the fingers of his right hand. Guess that answers it.

Audrey sits frozen, staring at the bone. The little girl, unhappy to have lost her new toy, grabs for the bone.

"No!" Audrey throws the bone away, so hard it flies right out of the grave and lands at her grandmother's feet. The baby starts screaming.

Mamie Lambert bends down—slowly, to make sure she'll be able to get back up—and picks up the bone. "What have we here? A bone?" She looks into the grave, at the Lambert tomb right next to it.

"I do believe we're leaking."

SIX

In the end, a group of firemen come to get the two youngest Lamberts out of the grave and the whole family takes off, taking the bone with them. I keep a close watch on Lebrun as they leave, wondering what would happen when one of his bones leaves the cemetery, but apart from a twitch in his right hand when they pass the gate, he shows no reaction.

We go back to waiting, Clothilde and I making our usual rounds in the cemetery and hanging out on her grave as is our habit, while Lebrun stays close to his own grave. He alternately stares down into the hole that hold his earthly remains and studies the Lambert grave, reading all the names and dates as if they hold the answer to some mystery.

On Wednesday, some middle-aged man comes to look at Lebrun's lot, apparently with the aim to buy it for his recently deceased wife.

On Thursday, one of the usual gravediggers drops by to inspect the empty grave, scraping at the wall closest to the Lambert tomb, shaking his head all the while. Then he opens several of the compartments of the Lambert grave and takes out pieces of God knows what to put them in little containers.

Two weeks later, the Lamberts are back. The same three women as the last time, but they've left the baby behind. Guess they don't want a repeat of their last visit.

Audrey carries a small package that we soon discover contains the bone from Lebrun's hand, and Sylvie carries a thick envelope. It all feels a lot more official than the usual family outings.

Clothilde takes a seat on the top of the Lambert tomb and for once I decide to join her, getting a perfect view of the assembly. Lebrun stands next to the Lambert women, his eyes on that first engraved name again.

"Well," Sylvie says to the package in her hand, "this is it. We're going to find out who you are and put you back where you belong."

"This family is weird," Clothilde says. "Anyone else would have just thrown the bone away or shoved it into any part of their tomb. Who cares which Lambert it belongs to?"

"To be fair, it doesn't belong to a Lambert."

Clothilde huffs a laugh. "Good point. What's in the envelope, do you think?"

I shrug. "Seems to be some proof of whose bone it is."

Giggles. "I wonder how far they'll throw the thing when they discover it's nobody from their family."

Lebrun has moved to stand next to Mamie Lambert. He's bending down to look into her wrinkled face, studying her from less than ten centimeters away. He studies her eyes, then goes so far as to reach out to let his ghostly finger pass through her nose, making the old lady sniff.

They're standing so close, facing each other, I suddenly have an epiphany. I haven't studied Lebrun's face too closely since he got here. His old-school clothes and hair draws my eye every time. But now that he's in profile, with Mamie's profile mirroring his.

"They have the same nose," I whisper.

Papers rustle and my attention is drawn to Sylvie when she exclaims, "What the hell does this mean?"

Audrey grabs the papers. "It's highly probable it's my great-grandfather…even more likely it's your grandfather…basically certain it's Mamie's dad. But…nothing in common with Pierre-Antoine Lambert."

"But…" Sylvie's mouth hangs open as she scans the pages for something that would make sense. "What does it mean? Didn't they bury the right body? Is grandfather's body buried somewhere else?"

Mamie Lambert doesn't seem to quite be following the conversation between her daughter and granddaughter. She's looking left and right, lifting her hand as if searching for something she cannot see.

Her hand passes through Lebrun's ghost several times, but the man doesn't move. He's staring at her face, mostly at her nose.

The same upturned nose as his.

The Lambert nose. Which appears to actually be the Lebrun nose.

"Uh," I start. I hesitate before deciding that I'm allowed to pry. "Lebrun, you wouldn't happen to have known Lambert's wife? Laetitia, wasn't it?"

Lebrun takes a step away from Mamie Lambert and dips his head just a fraction—I think it's his version of hanging his head. His eyes jump to the grave again, where Pierre-Antoine and Laetitia appear together at the top of the list.

"He'd been away for three years," he says in a defeated voice. "We'd been friends since we could walk and I'd always loved her. She married my friend instead, but once she got lonely during his absence…"

"Difficult to resist the woman you love, isn't it?"

Lebrun raises his hand to cover his eyes. I can see his lips trembling. "I know I shouldn't have done it. I deserve my punishment for what I did."

"Oh, is that why you stayed down there all this time?" Clothilde asks. "You thought you were doing penance?"

Lebrun doesn't answer but his expression is answer enough.

Sylvie and Audrey are still arguing, each with a wad of papers that she's shaking under the other woman's nose.

Mamie Lambert seems to snap out of her reverie. "It means Pierre-Antoine wasn't my real father, that's all. It was whoever this bone belongs to."

All eyes go to the little package with the bone.

"Who *does* it belong to?" Sylvie says to nobody in particular.

"It's from the grave next door!" Clothilde shouts at them.

Lebrun's eyebrows shoot up toward his hairline. He seems genuinely shocked by Clothilde's behavior.

I hope he won't have to stay long, because I don't think these two would be compatible over a longer period of time.

"Sometimes it helps talking to them," I explain. "They can't exactly hear us, but sometimes they do anyway."

As if on cue, Mamie points to the newly emptied grave. "Who was in that one, already?"

Sylvie emits a sigh, as if somebody poked her with a needle and all the air was leaking out. "I guess we'll have to find out."

ᴄ⳽

SOMEBODY MUST HAVE made the idiot gravediggers admit what they'd done because only days later a team of police experts came and dug up the bottom of Lebrun's grave. Without great surprise, they found what they were looking for. They put the bones in a casket and left the cemetery.

Once they passed the gate, Lebrun went with them, sitting on his new casket like some wound-up cowboy riding into the sunset.

SEVEN

HE COMES BACK a week later.

He has a brand new white and shining urn and the entire Lambert family attends his second funeral, this time in the Lambert family tomb.

"I still don't understand what happened," Sylvie says to Mamie Lambert as the urn is placed in its final resting place—let's hope for real, this time. "Your mother always forced on all of us how much she loved her husband. It's the reason we all come here every single week. And now we discover she wasn't even faithful?"

"That's probably why," Mamie replied calmly. "Guilt." She looks away for a moment—straight at Lebrun, who is once again standing right in front of her. In front of his daughter.

"I'm sure she loved Papa just as much as she said," Mamie finally says. "But she made a mistake while he was away and expressing her love for him and making his grave into a family shrine when he died was her way of repenting."

"I feel sorry for her," Audrey says, her voice low so that the rest of the family won't overhear. "Even if she did love Pierre-Antoine more, she must also have cared for this Lebrun guy. She lost both of them within a couple of months."

All heads nod in agreement and they finish the interment in silence.

☙

"SHE'S RIGHT, YOU know," Clothilde says to Lebrun once the Lambert family is gone. "The two of you died almost at the same time."

"There was a war in progress," Lebrun replies curtly. "Millions of people died that year."

"But you weren't at the war. And you died anyway. For an unknown reason."

Lebrun doesn't have an answer to that as he stands in front of his new grave, staring at the name of his one love. Is he going to stand there for the next hundred years?

"Apparently being buried with your actual family members isn't enough to let you move on," I say to Lebrun. "I'm honestly thinking you were murdered and you need the culprit to pay."

Lebrun stays silent, staring at the gilded letters.

"You know who the culprit is, don't you?" Clothilde asks as

she walks up to Lebrun so he'll at least see her in his peripheral vision. "She killed you when she learned her husband was coming home?"

Accepting that the love of his life didn't love him back. That she killed him to protect her own reputation. That would be a hard pill to swallow.

Could that be all he needed?

"Does it sound at all possible?" I ask him softly.

His face is as impassive as always, but I can see the moment the acceptance eases up some of the tightness of his features.

"Hey, at least you fathered a daughter," Clothilde chimes in, surprisingly compassionate. "Who had kids of her own, and so on all the way down to that baby who fell into your grave. They might have given thanks to the wrong guy for a century, but now they know you were at their origin, I'm sure they'll remember you in their own way during their family outings. That's not so bad."

Clothilde and I share a look. None of us ever have any visitors.

"I guess it could have been worse," Lebrun whispers. He grazes the name of Pierre-Antoine Lambert with his hand—and disappears.

HERITAGE

A Ghost Detective Short Story

BOOK 7

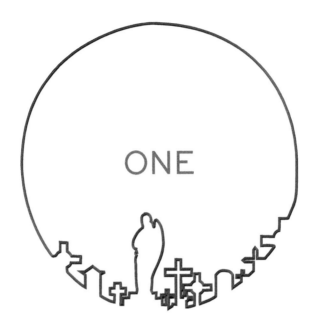

ONE

PLEASE SAVE ME from the chrysanthemums. Whoever nicknamed them the daisies of the dead better not come through here or we're going to have words.

I think I remember what they smell like, from long ago, when I still had a physical nose and a sense of smell. Not too sweet, not your typical flower smell. More like an herb, or the smell of fresh dirt.

Which is fitting for a cemetery, I guess.

But it's just too much. All year round our cemetery is monochrome. Most of the tombstones are granite, which can go from the clear gray of a November morning to the dark speckled gray of a starry midnight sky. Some of the older monuments are stone, which is why they're slowly crumbling, leaving the sculpted angels without hands, or with iron spikes sticking out of their wings. The paths are dark gray cobblestones or light gray gravel.

The only color comes from the few cypress trees on the north side of the cemetery and the rare flowers left by mourners. Mostly, the flowers are plastic.

But for two days a year, our cemetery turns into a loud rainbow. Blue, red, white, yellow, orange…you name a color, I can guarantee someone will find a corresponding chrysanthemum.

And they'll cover the family graves with them, and by cover, I mean *cover*. The Cordonnier family down by the well have a classic flat monument with a sober headstone showing names and dates of the deceased. On the Day of the Dead, you cannot even see the color of the monument and just barely make out the top of the headstone through the flowers. This year it's all blue.

The Perrots have opted for red and yellow and they've set the chrysanthemums up in the shape of a cross, one big enough to take on a life-size Jesus.

Not all cemeteries get this much attention, but this particular village seems to have gone a little crazy at one point in history and now can't figure out how to get back to normal. I guess if everybody else's grave is covered in colorful flowers, you don't want to be the *one* family who neglects to come pay your respects to the dead.

Clothilde and I, of course, *have* the two graves where nobody ever places any flowers. Well, Clothilde does, anyway. I don't even have a tombstone to mark the place I'm buried.

Clothilde's last resting place is marked by a simple slab of local white-and-gray granite—the cheapest one available, if I'm not mistaken—and a classic headstone with only her first name and date of death.

The woman herself is now perching on her headstone, her hands under her jeans-clad thighs and her Converse-clad feet gliding through the granite as she swings her feet back and forth. Clothilde has been a ghost for long enough to master the art of deciding which rules of the world of the living to follow. Having a stone to sit on: yes. Having it stop her from dangling her legs: nope.

Her intelligent eyes sweep the cemetery as she shakes her head. "Can't we try telling them they're here on the wrong day? Maybe one of them is sensitive enough to listen?"

"And you think the rest of these crazy people will listen in turn?"

We have this discussion every year. Being ghosts stuck in a cemetery for almost thirty years, we have time to spare, of course, but we're not going to come to any transcending conclusions today either.

In France, the first of November—today—is Toussaint, the All Saints' Day. The second of November is the Day of the Dead, when you're supposed to go to the cemetery to honor the dead and pray for their redemption. The problem is that the first is a public holiday and the second isn't. So little by little, the tradition of coming to the cemetery—with chrysanthemums—has moved over to the first.

"Even if they did hear us," I say to Clothilde from my spot sitting cross-legged on the little bump next to her grave that marks my spot, "it would just mean that they show up a day later. They'd still come at some point. We'd still be flooded with the flowers."

"It *would* be better," Clothilde grumbles. "The people who work tomorrow wouldn't be able to come."

"And a bunch of dead people wouldn't get visits from their families, wouldn't have prayers said for them."

Clothilde rolls her eyes in true teenager fashion. "They don't care. They're dead. And not ghosts. Not anymore, anyway."

Clothilde and I have made it our mission to help the ghosts who come through our cemetery to move on. We don't know where they go—obviously, since we're still here ourselves—but we're convinced it's a better place.

Not everyone becomes a ghost, only the people with unfinished business. It can be as simple as not having said goodbye to a loved one, not having apologized for that one regretful act, or it can be needing justice when someone is murdered and the killer isn't caught.

Solving murders from within the confines of a cemetery when nobody can see or hear you is something of a challenge, but we manage. So far, everybody coming through here as a ghost has moved on.

Except for the two of us, of course.

"The mom at the Tessier grave is here," Clothilde says, tilting her head toward the section with the most recent graves. "She brought roses again."

I stand up to have a better look. The woman buried her son here about six months ago and we've been seeing her every week, without fail.

Can't say I blame her. No parent should ever have to bury their child and the younger they were when they passed away, the worse it is. Daniel Tessier had just turned eighteen.

He never became a ghost, though. So he didn't have any unfinished business. But it seems like his mom does. Not that we know what it is because the woman never speaks. She just sits there, kneeling at her son's grave, staring at his name on the headstone.

"I'm going over to check on her," I say.

Clothilde sighs but jumps down from her perch to follow. "You're not going to get her to talk just because it's the Day of the Dead. Because it's *not* the Day of the Dead. It's All Saints' Day!" She yells the last part across the cemetery.

She gets no reaction from the living, of course.

As we reach her, Madame Tessier is running her fingers over the bright red petals of the roses she brought for her son's grave. Her gaze keeps shifting between the roses and the yellow and orange chrysanthemums of the neighboring grave. Did she not know about the tradition?

"The roses are lovely," I tell her. "A welcome change for those of us who live here."

She doesn't hear me, of course. They never do. But from time to time, we get visitors who are more sensitive to ghosts than most and we can influence them in small ways. Give them ideas that they'll think were their own. Make their skin crawl with the feeling that someone's watching.

That particular feature hasn't actually come in handy to solve any cases. But when she's in the right mood, Clothilde has some fun with it.

Madame Tessier seems more upset than I'd consider normal at the fact that she didn't bring the right type of flowers. She sits back on her heels and looks around the cemetery—probably really seeing the rest of it for the first time—taking in the explosion of color.

"Why is she crying about the flowers?" Clothilde squats down on her haunches to study the woman's face from up close. "There's nothing wrong with your roses, Madame. They're lovely. And probably smell a lot better than that other crap."

Two lonely tears are indeed making their way down the woman's cheeks.

I spot another woman, one I can't remember seeing before, just two graves down. She has put a large pot of purple flowers—yes, yes, chrysanthemums, what else—on the grave of Monsieur and Madame Bartoli. Given their ages and hers, I guess she *might* be a daughter or niece.

Since the woman at the Bartoli grave is already sending worried glances at Madame Tessier, I walk over and talk directly into her ear. "You should go over and tell her that the roses are lovely. She looks like she might need a hug."

Clothilde seems to have come to the same conclusion. She's caressing Madame Tessier's cheek, attempting to swipe the tears away. For a tough-as-nails teenager with a constant I-don't-care attitude, this show of affection is startling.

The Bartoli woman seems to have heard me, bless her. She walks over to the Tessier grave and clears her throat. "Lovely roses," she says in a soft tone. She takes in the dates on the headstone and the picture of a young man next to it. "I'm sorry for your loss, Madame."

Madame Tessier twitches as if brought back to reality. She wipes a hand over her cheek to bat away the tears, hitting Clothilde through the head while she's at it. "Thank you," she says in a wavering voice. "I, uh…I didn't realize today was special." She waves a hand at the rest of the colorful cemetery. "I'm not… not from around here."

The Bartoli woman smiles serenely. "Today is special for the dead who are mostly forgotten the rest of the year. Do not feel guilty for thinking of your lost ones more often than when tradition dictates."

Madame Tessier sighs and sinks lower on her heels. Little by little the air seems to be going out of her and I just hope she'll have the energy to get home safely when she's finished communing with her son.

"My daughter just turned sixteen," the Bartoli woman says.

Her eyes on the picture of her son, Madame Tessier just nods. "He's not here," she says after a while.

"Who?"

"My son. They say he's buried here but I don't believe it. I can't feel him at all. I don't think the body they found in that incinerated dumpster was his."

Clothilde jumps up on the neighboring headstone to perch there. "Well, she's not wrong about him not being here. We never saw the guy."

I can't remember seeing this before. We've had lots of ghosts who want to communicate and reach out to the living but not the other way around. And certainly not when the deceased didn't even become a ghost.

The Bartoli woman doesn't seem to know what to say after that and silently slips away toward the parking lot.

Madame Tessier stays at her son's grave until all the other families have left and the security guard accompanies her to the gate. She never says a word.

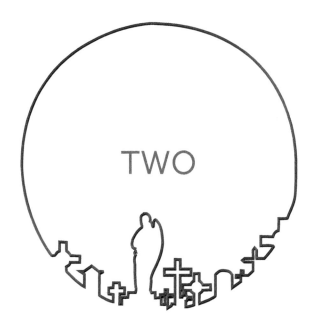

TWO

THAT NIGHT, WE get something new.

In the past few years, we've seen kids getting dressed up and going door to door trick-or-treating. Back when I was alive in the eighties, this wasn't part of the Toussaint celebration in France but something we heard about from across the Atlantic. Now the tradition seems to be inserting itself into French society as well.

In the afternoon, we see the kids with their sugar. At night, it's the teenagers and students—with their alcohol.

My inner police officer winces every time I see these groups. They're drinking too much, wearing too little clothing, not always making sure nobody's left behind. I once saw a girl who couldn't be more than sixteen stagger down the street running along the south wall of the cemetery, wearing nothing but what appeared to be a bloody nurse's uniform with a *lot* of pieces missing and clearly not in a state to take herself home. I wanted to help her, I wanted to call someone who could actually help, I wanted to yell at her friends for abandoning her.

But as a ghost I couldn't do any of those things.

Tonight, it seems like someone wanted to up the stakes. At five minutes past midnight, a witch's hat appears over the south wall, in the spot where the ivy covers it completely, quickly followed by the rest of the witch. She's wearing all black, has long dark hair and enough makeup to make her look seventy instead of probably-nineteen. She jumps the wall and lands on our side with a little squeak and a stumble—yep, she's drunk.

"It's all clear!" she whisper-yells across the wall.

"What the hell is going on?" Clothilde asks. We're standing on the Jacquier family tomb, watching the new arrivals. "Who breaks into a cemetery at midnight?"

"Someone who wants an extra thrill on the Night of the Dead."

Three more heads appear over the wall and with various levels of expertise draw themselves over the wall and through the ivy, to land next to the witch. We have one nun with fake blood pouring out of a slit throat, one zombie who's either very good at imitating the walk of a zombie or very drunk, and one—

"Is that girl dressed as a garden gnome?"

Baggy dark clothing, a red fluffy cap, huge fake beard, large black combat boots, and a heavy backpack. "That…uh…yeah, maybe weird garden gnome."

The gnome seems to be in charge. "All right," she says in a voice tense with excitement. "Let's split up. Whoever starts running or screaming first loses. Selfies in front of at least six graves from different parts of the cemetery. And make it look good and scary, yeah?"

The zombie, who's listing at a fifteen-degree angle, pats himself down, I assume in search of a phone. He ends up finding it in a back pocket and takes an inordinate amount of time to extricate it. "Goddit," he slurs. And ambles off in the direction of the church.

The nun and the witch exchange a glance. "Let's start down there?" The nun nods her head in the exact opposite direction of where the zombie went.

"Nuh-huh." The gnome adjusts her backpack and I can hear the clinking of glass. Is she carrying the alcohol of the entire group in there? "We go separately. Otherwise it won't be as scary. And we won't see any ghosts."

Clothilde chuckles. "They want to see ghosts, do they?" Her eyes gleam with anticipated glee. "Can I play? Please, Robert, can I play?"

I can't decide what to think of the situation. The idea of teenagers coming into a cemetery at midnight in the search of ghosts feels…ludicrous. Who still believes in ghosts at that age?

Then again…there *are* actually two ghosts here and we're most definitely real.

And the idea of messing with the kids—because, of course, they don't actually believe in ghosts, they just want to give themselves a good scare—is quite tempting.

"Okay," I tell Clothilde. "We'll follow them around and see what opportunities come up. But no scaring so somebody actually gets hurt, you hear me?"

Predictably, Clothilde rolls her eyes. "Yes, *Dad*."

There's a short argument between the three girls, but the gnome ends up getting her way. They split up, each going toward a different part of the cemetery.

"I wanna mess with the nun," Clothilde says, and takes off after the girl in question.

I'm more intrigued by the gnome, so I decide to follow her. She seems to be a lot less drunk than her friends but still clearly the instigator of this nightly outing. She's also *not at all* looking for ghosts. She walks past looming mausoleums without so much as a glance inside, doesn't spare a second thought to the rotting iron door that's squeaking on its hinges in tonight's slight breeze, and barely even notices the stone angel with only half a head and skeletal wings that people tend to stay away from even in broad daylight.

This girl in on a mission.

Her head *does* whip around when a scream sounds across the cemetery. It's followed by loud cackling but I'm the only one who can hear it—I'd recognize Clothilde anywhere. Guess she managed to give the nun a good scare.

"Seriously?" the gnome girl mutters, hitches her backpack higher on her shoulders, and keeps going. When she passes the Beauvois chapel, her clear eyes dart inside.

I'll admit to considering the possibility of doing like Clothilde and playing with the girl—until I remember I'm a grown man and a police officer to boot. Spooking kids in a cemetery really should be beneath me.

The gnome girl comes to a stop—in front of the Tessier grave.

She dumps her backpack on the ground and opens it to pull out a *shovel* of all things. Please tell me she's not going to vandalize the grave of the poor Tessier boy. The mother has suffered enough as it is.

She walks around the grave with the shovel, studying the granite and the ground around it. She definitely wants in. Why?

After two rounds, she gives up. There's no way for a person to get into that grave without some serious tools. A small spade certainly isn't going to do the trick.

So she starts branching out. Leaving the backpack at the Tessier grave, she ambles past the neighboring graves, looking into the ones with chapels, going behind the large ones, apparently hoping for a hidden entrance.

Then she gets to the newest grave. The one that doesn't host a casket or a body yet.

We don't know who's coming, of course, but *someone* died recently and their grave is being readied. They came in two days ago to dig the hole and I expect the funeral to take place within the week.

Another scream pierces the night. This time it's definitely male and coming from a different part of the cemetery. Clothilde has decided to have fun with all of them.

The gnome girl looks up and frowns in the direction of the scream but doesn't stay distracted for long. She seems happy with the empty grave. She goes to get her backpack and proceeds to empty it.

First three empty beer bottles. Then several heavy black plastic bags.

"What you got in there, little gnome?" I ask her. I'm not liking the looks of this.

A flash goes off somewhere nearby. I think I see the witch girl over by the scary angel statue—she's working on their selfie challenge. Clothilde is standing right next to her—a shame she won't show up in the picture—talking into the girl's ear but from the lack of reaction, I'm guessing this girl isn't sensitive to supernatural activities at all.

The gnome girl stays perfectly still, crouching by the open grave, and waits for her friend to move on. When she's alone, she dumps the contents of one of the plastic bags on the ground.

It's a leg.

THREE

I STAND FROZEN in shock as the girl lumps the leg into the open grave and proceeds to do the same with the contents of the remaining bags. I count two lower legs with feet—I'd say male from the size and body hair—two thighs, and two arms.

Something seems off about them at first. As I take a closer look, I realize they're frozen. They're not as soft and malleable as I'd expect skin and flesh to be. These legs and arms were in a freezer not so long ago.

I try to get a better look at the girl, as if seeing her facial features clearly will allow this situation to make more sense. She's white, she has blond hair, but I don't know if it's short or long because of the beanie, and the eyes seem clear though I can't determine the exact color in the dark. Most of her face is covered by the fake beard so I can't even tell the general shape of her face.

When she starts shoveling dirt into the grave to cover the body parts, I run to get Clothilde. She's standing over a cowering nun at the foot of one of the cypress trees, a faintly regretful expression on her pretty face.

"I may have gone too far with this one," she says. "I'm trying to tell her I'm not dangerous and that she's safe here but it's not working as well as the scary stuff."

"Just leave her alone and she'll be fine," I say. "I need you to come with me."

A quick glance at my face and she doesn't even question me. Clothilde *can* be serious when necessary.

When we reach the open grave, the gnome girl has finished covering up the body parts and has shoved the empty plastic bags into her backpack. She's posing for a selfie in front of one of the neighboring graves, wearing a smile that the circumstances make scary as hell.

"She just dumped a pair of arms and legs into that open grave," I tell Clothilde. "This *teenager* killed some guy and is getting rid of the body in our cemetery."

Clothilde jumps into the grave to have a look. As a ghost, she can't dig in the dirt but it seems not all the parts are completely covered. "That's a man's *foot*," she says. I think it's the first time I see my friend genuinely shocked.

The gnome girl finishes taking her pictures and I watch over her shoulder as she sends messages to her friends that it's time to meet up at the spot where they came over the wall.

Then she walks over to the open grave. The venom in her voice surprises me as she says to the buried body parts, "Now you stay here, you hear me?"

I exchange a look with Clothilde. "Interesting."

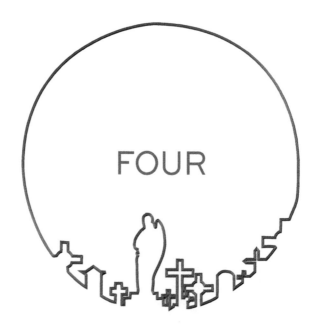

FOUR

SHE COMES BACK twice during the night—without her friends but with the gnome outfit still on—first with the upper part of the torso, then with the rest and the head.

"It's that Tessier boy, isn't it?" Clothilde says calmly as she studies the head before it's covered with dirt.

"Seems likely," I reply. "That's where she originally wanted to bury him." We've both been down in the grave since the girl's second trip in a vain attempt to accompany this poor soul during his below-par funeral.

"What is this dump?" I nearly jump out of my nonexistent skin when the angry male voice speaks. "You're not going to leave me here. You're not getting away with this."

"This time you're staying," the gnome girl says through gritted teeth as she shovels more dirt into the hole. "You're not going to bother me ever again."

Clothilde and I hurry out of the grave, me pretending there are stairs to step on and Clothilde not bothering and floating up like a proper ghost. There, leaning over the gnome girl, is the ghost of a young man, his face contorted in anger as he's hissing insults in her ear.

"*Is* that the Tessier boy?"

"I think so," I say. Though it's difficult to link the features of this angry ghost with those of the innocent-looking boy in the picture on the Tessier grave.

The gnome girl can clearly hear the ghost on a certain level because she flinches when he yells at her or touches her, but she keeps working, keeps focused on her task.

"Shouldn't we stop him?" Clothilde asks. "I'm not above a little poking now and then but this guy is too much."

"I'm pretty sure she's the one who killed him, which is why he's a ghost and she's getting rid of his body in a cemetery in the middle of the night."

"Oh. Right." Clothilde cocks her head. "Should we help *him*?"

I shake my head. "I don't like the way he's behaving either. Something's not adding up. We'll talk to him when she leaves."

"But what if he leaves with her?"

I wave at the body parts scattered in the open grave. "His entire body is here now. He's going to be as stuck within these walls as we are. I wonder how the girl figured out this would be the right way to get rid of him."

We never get the chance to know. When she has covered the bottom of the grave with enough dirt and gravel for it to look approximately as even as it was earlier, she grabs her tools and practically sprints to the ivy-covered wall.

Ghost boy sprints after her—I notice he's fresh enough to reflexively follow the rules of the physical realm rather than just flying after her—yelling all the way.

Like I predicted, he's unable to follow over the wall.

"Should we go talk to him?" Clothilde asks as we stand there looking at the boy yelling insults at the gnome girl, at the wall, at the universe.

"Let's give him a couple of minutes to calm down first."

FIVE

It takes him a couple of hours but in the end he calms down enough for us to approach him.

"Good evening, young man," I say to him and have the satisfaction of seeing him jump in fright. "Welcome to our cemetery."

The poor guy shimmers for a few seconds, to the point where I can see straight through him. "You...you're ghosts?"

I look down at myself and at Clothilde. We're all shades of gray without a speck of color. We're not really transparent but also not solid. Clothilde has jumped up to perch on the wall and is dangling her feet through the wall as per usual. "Yes," I reply, just to make sure we don't lose more time than necessary. "We're ghosts. As are you. I'm Robert and this is Clothilde."

At first he just stands there, his mouth hanging open. Then he snaps out of it. "Nathan," he says. "Nathan Tessier."

"Ah, yes. We've met your mother."

"You—you have? My mom's dead?" He suddenly looks five years younger and completely lost.

"No! She's alive and well, I assure you. But she comes to visit your grave quite often."

"My *grave*? My body was just dumped at the bottom of a hole that I'm pretty sure was never meant for me."

"Oh. Right." I turn to look in the direction of the Tessier grave and scratch my head, not that I can feel it. "I wonder whose body is in there." Probably some poor homeless person who was in the wrong place at the wrong time.

Clothilde snorts, followed by an "Oops" and then a "Sorry" in Nathan's direction.

We show Nathan the Tessier grave, with his name and photo and the latest batch of roses. Nathan notices that all the other graves have different flowers and runs his hand through the red petals. "She always loved red roses." Shaking his head, he turns to me. "How long has this been here?"

I point to the date on the headstone. "About six months. Your mother comes by at least once a week. Earlier today she claimed she couldn't feel you here, that you weren't in that grave. Which I find interesting, considering."

"How did you die?" Clothilde asks.

"How did I—?" I can see the anger rising in him like a tidal wave. "That—that—" He points a shaking hand in the direction of the ivy-covered wall.

"The gnome girl," I offer.

He snorts a laugh, and his anger recedes just enough for him to find words. "She hit me over the head with a bottle! She *killed* me. Then she shoved my entire body into an empty freezer she had in the basement and left me there for *months*."

"Is that where you became a ghost?" Clothilde says. "Instead of rising from a casket, you rose from a freezer?"

Nathan shrugs. "At first I was stuck in there, but at some point I could get out of the freezer but was still stuck in the house."

"Which is when you started to haunt gnome girl." No wonder she needed to get rid of him.

"Well…yeah. What else was I supposed to do?"

Good point.

"She just hit you over the head with a bottle? For no reason?" Clothilde paces by the neighboring grave. I'm guessing she wants to sit on it but doesn't want to get too close to the chrysanthemums.

"Well…yeah."

I use the oldest questioning technique in the book: silence.

And it works like a charm. "I mean, we were having an argument, all right? We were both really angry, and then, bam! I'm dead."

"Mhmm." Clothilde eyes our new arrival, sizing him up. He's taller than me and seems to be in good shape. The gnome girl wasn't exactly weak—she managed to carry this guy's body here, after all—but she was quite small.

"What were you arguing about?" I ask him.

He huffs. "You know. Couple's stuff."

Clothilde's eyebrows shoot up. "She was your *girlfriend*?"

"She was until five minutes before I died."

SIX

WE DON'T GET anything else out of him for the rest of the night. We go back to Clothilde's grave and let Nathan take in the site of his own tombstone in peace.

The next day, the actual Day of the Dead, his mother returns.

The weather is as gray and sad as yesterday, with the breeze having picked up some speed and heavy clouds in the west promising rain in the near future. Nathan's mother is wearing her usual jeans and black sneakers, with a dark purple raincoat.

She brings a pot of yellow chrysanthemums.

"Mom!" Nathan says when she arrives at his grave.

Madame Tessier, who hasn't reacted at all when we've tried

talking to her during her visits, who I would have declared as completely insensitive to ghosts, turns her head in her son's direction. "Nathan?"

"Oh shit," Clothilde says. We've approached to observe but keep out of the conversation, at least for the moment. And there *is* a conversation, which is astounding.

"Mom, you have to help me. You have to get Mélanie. She *killed* me, Mom. She put me in the freezer and cut my body into pieces and now dumped me *here*. She can't get away with it, Mom."

Tears are forming in Madame Tessier's eyes. "I'm so happy you're finally here, Nathan. I was worried I wouldn't be able to help you find peace."

"Huh," I say. "Looks like we're getting help this time."

"What do you think he needs to move on?" Clothilde asks.

"Murder victims usually need the murderer to be caught."

"Mhmm."

"You have to go find Mélanie," Nathan pleads with his mom. "She used her father's tools to cut up my body and just cleaned them in the bathroom sink before taking them back out to the garage. Get the cops over there today, Mom."

Madame Tessier cocks her head to the side as if trying to make something out. She's the most sensitive person I've ever seen but I don't think she's hearing her son's actual words. It's probably more of a general feeling.

"It was because of Mélanie, wasn't it?" she says finally. The sadness in her tone surprises me. Lowering her head, she says, "I knew I should have left earlier."

Nathan looks about as confused as I feel.

Madame Tessier scans the cemetery. An elderly couple is setting up some flowers on a grave close to the church but otherwise the place is deserted. "I saw the signs," she says with a faraway look in her eyes. "But I didn't act. I was so used to looking the other way and finding excuses that I didn't stop and think what it was doing *to you.*

"When you were kicked out of your first school, I blamed the teachers. They simply didn't know how to channel your energy. When you weren't allowed to continue karate…well, I was too absorbed in healing my own visible wounds to worry about your invisible ones.

"And when you hit that teacher… That's when I realized I had to get us out. But it was already too late, wasn't it?"

"What's she talking about?" Clothilde whispers.

"I'm guessing an abusive husband with anger management issues," I reply.

Nathan seems to be frozen on the spot. He's back to looking twelve instead of eighteen. He's like a lost little boy.

"I'm guessing you hit Mélanie?" Madame Tessier says sadly. She sighs. "Such a sweet girl. But easily distracted, wasn't she? Can probably get annoying fast. For you."

"She never finished a sentence," Nathan whispers. "She'd start one sentence and then finish another one."

Madame Tessier runs a hand over the flowers she brought for her son's grave. "Can't believe that little girl had the guts to do what I never managed." She swallows. "You have to understand that this isn't her fault, *chéri*. Nor is it yours. It's your father's, for teaching you the wrong way to manage your emotions. And mine, for not getting you away soon enough.

"I'm sorry, Nathan. I hope you'll finally find peace now." She pushes the roses from yesterday a little to the side so that they're just below the picture of her son.

And she leaves.

⋘

I PLAN TO let Nathan be for a while after his mother leaves but when I see him turning translucent I realize he's ready to move on.

"You all right, Nathan?" I ask him as I approach where he's sitting on his own grave running his hands through the roses. "Looks like you've found the closure you needed to move on."

He holds up his hand. It's see-through. "It's not my fault," he says with wonder in his voice. And disappears.

I join Clothilde at the freshly dug grave currently housing the defrosting and dismembered body of Nathan Tessier. "You think we should help someone notice that there's an extra body down there?"

We could. When they come with whoever that grave is for, we should be able to find someone sensitive enough for us to give them the thought that the grave doesn't seem quite as deep as it should be. They'll find the body parts and chances are the young Mélanie didn't cover her tracks well enough and get arrested.

Neither mother nor son seemed to actually need for the girl to get caught to get closure.

"I think just this once, we'll not interfere."

NEW BEGINNINGS

A Ghost Detective Short Story

BOOK 8

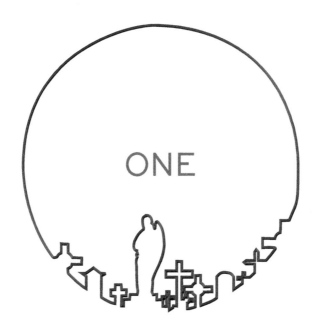

ONE

EVERYBODY DIES ALONE, they say.

No matter how surrounded you are by family and friends in your life, no matter how rich or poor you are, no matter your social status, we're all equal—and alone—in death. Nobody can walk that path with you.

I don't remember my own death, so I find it hard to argue the point, facts in hand.

But I don't like to think that whoever came up with that saying was right.

I can't speak for what happens at the exact moment when someone dies, but I *can* tell you that none of the people who come through our cemetery as ghosts are ever alone.

Clothilde and I are always here to help them adjust to being ghosts, and to help them move on once they've settled whatever unfinished business made them linger.

If either of us ever moves on without the other, whoever remains will, indeed, be lonely. It's something I don't think about all that much anymore—we've both been here for more than thirty years, after all. Chances of either of us figuring out what we need to move on tomorrow are, quite frankly, slim.

It's been the two of us for such a long time, I've come to think of ghosts as belonging in two groups: us and them. Clothilde and I are the constants. The others are only passing through.

When other ghosts come through, we make the effort to get to know them. But we keep a distance, one that we need for our own well-being.

The first years in our cemetery, I befriended most of the other ghosts. Got to know them. What they liked, their sense of humor, their tastes and opinions.

And then they moved on, and left me behind.

Only Clothilde stayed.

So even though the rebellious twenty-year-old with wild, curly hair and worn Converse doesn't seem like the likely friend of a balding thirty-five-year-old washed-out cop, we're the closest thing either of us has to a family.

We're *us*.

And together, we welcome new ghosts—while keeping the required emotional distance.

Today, I think we have a new arrival.

I say *think*, because the signs aren't as clear as usual.

When someone has unfinished business and becomes a ghost, they wake up inside their casket sometime between the ceremony in the church and the moment when the church doors open. Without much surprise, when someone wakes up and discovers they are stuck in a sealed casket, they panic.

Usually, they scream—*we* scream, I was no exception—and pound on the casket, trying to get someone to save them.

This is what alerts us to new arrivals. The large wooden doors to our little stone church squeal open, the mourners pour out and wait on the small area in front of the church, huddling under shared umbrellas if the weather is as wet and depressing as it is today, and then the casket is carried out. Accompanied by screams if the person has become a ghost.

I *think* someone's yelling—but with the murmurs of the large group, the staccato *plops* of rain on umbrellas and gravestones, and the ringing of the church bells, I just can't be sure.

I can't even rule out the possibility of the yells coming from one of the mourners because the rain, the umbrellas, and a large number of hoods make all the people look blurry. This winter has been as depressing as they usually are in this part of France; rain, gray skies, and more rain. Every single day. Not even a single snowflake to brighten things up for a moment or two.

Now that it's finally March, maybe we'll get some sun and fresh spring.

"Is it possible to be too lazy to panic properly when you die?" Clothilde perches on the headstone of her own grave, her feet swinging back and forth, passing through the stone as if it weren't there, her head cocked as she listens for the yells.

"Maybe the rain muffles the sound," I say without conviction. I'm sitting on the small mound marking my own final resting place, very happy that ghosts can't get their pants wet, or feel the cold.

"The rain doesn't muffle ghost sounds," Clothilde replies, but without her usual snark. She's too focused on the casket.

Biting her cheek, she stretches her neck, as if that would help her see anything better from across the cemetery. "I think it's someone old. All the young people are clearly family. If anybody is a friend, they're at least eighty."

That information is probably not *quite* right. Clothilde may have been on this earth for over fifty years—twenty as a normal girl and thirty as a ghost—but her capacity for estimating the age of someone over forty leaves something to be desired.

But as I get up to get a better look myself, I have to concede the point. None of the "friend" mourners are a day under seventy.

"Let's get a little closer," I say, and start walking toward the hole where the casket is to be buried. It's an existing grave in one of the old and fancy parts of the cemetery. The granite slab was removed yesterday to prepare for today's funeral.

I take the narrow paths winding past the gray tombs, glancing at some graves with fresh flowers and regretfully noting the ones that haven't been cleaned in several decades.

Clothilde follows behind while cutting a few corners. She was never one for following the rules of the living when it doesn't suit her. The grave of Monsieur Lopez she cuts through on purpose, like she always does when going through that zone. He spent some time with us as a ghost. Clothilde did not like him.

The burial in itself is pretty straightforward so I don't even bother listening to what the priest says. I go down to crouch down on the casket six feet under to make sure that the sounds I'm hearing are coming from inside.

Polite knocking and the occasional, "Hello? Does anybody hear me?"

Well, that's new.

"Definitely a new arrival, and a polite one at that," I tell Clothilde as I join her in the crowd of mourners.

"There's something weird about this death," Clothilde says. She stands in the middle of the crowd, her hands on her hips, and studies everyone in the vicinity. "And there's something weird about the mourners."

I take the time to look, too. She's right. There's something off about the people around us—but I can't put my finger on what it is.

"What do you mean, there's something weird about the death?" I ask. "From what I understand, the woman was seventy-three, and her husband died and was buried here ten years ago." I find it highly unlikely that the newly arrived Madame Priaux was a murder victim, for example.

Clothilde moves toward a lone woman in her thirties standing somewhat apart from the group in the back. Tears are streaking down her face and this has clearly been going on for a while. Her cheeks are as wet as her raincoat, making it look like the hood has no effect whatsoever.

Clothilde scrutinizes the woman from head to foot several times. "They're too upset."

I fight the urge to roll my eyes—that's usually Clothilde's favorite way of expressing herself. "People are allowed to be upset when they lose someone they love."

Frowning, Clothilde leans in so close to the woman that their noses almost touch. "Not this much. Not for a woman in her seventies who's 'joining her husband.' Not for people who have already lost grandparents, so they know what it's like." She leans back and meets my gaze. "They're shocked this woman is dead."

I make a quick tour around the people present. And conclude that Clothilde is right.

"Maybe it's a familial or cultural thing. They don't deal well with loss?"

Clothilde's reply is a snort. At least she didn't roll her eyes.

The ceremony finished, people mill towards their cars. The young, sad woman remains, and is joined by a man who might be in his early forties. His hair is thinning on top and completely gray around the ears. His beer belly strains his coat around the waist and his black umbrella only covers his front. The back of his jacket is soaked, as are his legs from the knees down.

"Come now, cousin," he says to the woman. "No need to beat yourself up. You did the best you could. It was her time." He holds the umbrella away with one arm and reaches out the other toward the woman's shoulder, clearly to lean in to kiss her cheek.

The woman steps away. "Don't! I might have it."

The man sighs. "You didn't have any symptoms while you were with Mamie for a week, you haven't had any since she died. You're fine. Let me give you a kiss and some human contact. *That* is what we need when we're mourning."

The woman doesn't seem convinced but her cousin doesn't give her much choice. He leans in and kisses her cheek, then retreats back under his umbrella.

"Come," he says to her. "You need to get out of the rain. Can't have you catching your death in this weather." He guffaws at his own joke.

"She died from some kind of contagious disease?" Clothilde says when the two cousins leave the cemetery. "What, like, the flu?"

I can only shrug. We're in France, a country with health care for all and mandatory vaccines. I have to agree with Clothilde. The flu is the only common contagious disease I can think of that would kill an elderly lady like this.

"If that was the flu, then I'll eat a rat," says a shaky voice from behind us.

We rush over to the grave, and find an elderly lady with curled gray hair and thick-rimmed glasses with rhinestones along the top staring up at us, hands on hips.

"Would either of you young people mind telling me how I get out of this pit?"

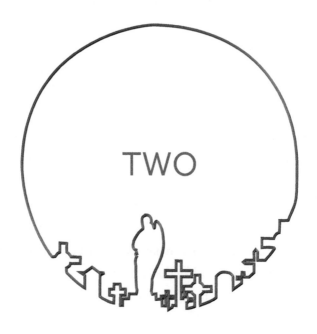

TWO

HER NAME IS Marie-Pierre and she's seventy-three. She used to be a teller in a bank, something she took a break from for fifteen years to raise three children, and eventually went back to when she started feeling claustrophobic in her own home. She has seven grandchildren, one of whom is in great danger of making her a great-grandmother very soon if she doesn't watch out.

"So how did you die?" Clothilde asks. Marie-Pierre didn't feel comfortable sitting on someone else's grave and her own isn't really an option right now, so we've settled on one of the benches under the plane trees. Clothilde is sprawled on the wet ground, ignoring the rain completely, her jeans-clad legs stretched long and arms propped behind her for unneeded support. I'm on the bench with our new colleague, keeping a polite distance.

Marie-Pierre waves a hand in the air. "Some kind of virus. I think. I was quite out of it when they took me to the hospital and although I know they talked about whatever it was around and over me, I didn't really listen." She gets a faraway look and the wrinkles on her forehead deepen. "I was too busy fighting to breathe."

We sit in silence for a while. I have more questions for Maire-Pierre but we're hardly in a rush. She was surprisingly quick to come out of the casket, which might be linked to her age. At some point, people know the end is coming, so it's easier to accept when it happens. Not that seventy-three means a foot in the grave. Rather…well, death is closer than it was yesterday.

"I don't suppose Noël is around?" Marie-Pierre twists around on her bench, scanning the cemetery.

That's the name that was already on the grave Marie-Pierre was buried in. "Was he your husband?" I ask.

"Yes. He died ten years ago. Heart attack from doing too much sport after he retired." She sighs and smiles wistfully. "My mother always told me he was stupid."

"I'm afraid we're the only resident ghosts at this time," I tell her. "Not everybody becomes a ghost, you see. And those who do, don't always linger very long."

Her sharp gaze, too serious for the ridiculous glasses she wears, catches mine. "Yet you've been here for some time."

"Yes. I have." I leave it at that. "Your husband never became a ghost. He must have moved on directly, like the majority of people do. He must not have had any unfinished business."

"Not other than getting up that mountain on his brand new bike," she grumbles. She glances at Clothilde, then back at me. "You are insinuating that I *do* have unfinished business? That's why I'm here?"

Clothilde sits up, wrapping her arms around her knees. "Do you know what it might be?"

Marie-Pierre takes her time thinking about it, cocking her head left and right, grimacing and mumbling to herself.

Finally, she shrugs and folds her hands in her lap. "Nope. Not a clue."

THREE

We expect Marie-Pierre to get visitors once the grave is sealed. Quite often, the people our ghosts have unfinished business with come back, because it's a two-way street.

For two days, not a soul comes to visit—not Marie-Pierre nor anybody else.

On the third day, we get another funeral.

With another new arrival.

This time, there's no doubt. As the church doors open, the screams blow out of the church, loud and male and angry. The pounding on the casket is constant and with several different kinds of resonance—this guy is hitting with both hands and feet. Today, miraculously, there's no rain, so we hear everything perfectly.

"Oh, my," Marie-Pierre says as she slips her glasses down her nose to study the spectacle over their rim. I've tried to explain that she doesn't need glasses anymore, and certainly shouldn't have trouble with focusing on something far away, but the woman just shrugged and adjusted her glasses.

Some habits are hard to kick—and some we don't want to.

We watch from afar as the casket is carried to a newly dug grave in the northeast section and the priest makes a quick sermon.

"Not too many people this time," Clothilde comments. She has abandoned her usual perch to stand on the other side of Marie-Pierre, her arms crossed across her chest and a slight frown on her face.

"Huh," Marie-Pierre says as she yet again lowers her glasses to look at the mourners. "That *is* odd."

"Why?" I ask. We're supposed to be the specialists on funerals and mourners here, not the new arrival.

She points a bony finger at the family standing closest to the grave. A woman in her late fifties and two twenty-something men. They're all blond and stocky.

"That's Lisa and her weird sons. If Didier isn't with her, it means he's the one in the casket." She cocks her head. "Yes, that definitely sounds like Didier." She sends me a look that I'm unable to decipher. "Didier is one of the village's three doctors. He was *my* doctor."

She stops talking but the conversation is clearly continuing in her head. I also see her counting out the number of mourners and mumbling names.

"Everybody loved Didier," she finally says. "He was loud and smart and funny. The entire village should have come to his funeral." She waves at the twenty-five people around the open grave. "This is only family."

I meet Clothilde's gaze over Marie-Pierre's head but my friend just shrugs at me. Village chatter doesn't interest Clothilde.

"Did his family get along well?" I've suddenly realized what seemed odd to *me* about this group—and I think it was the case during Marie-Pierre's funeral, too. "They're not standing very close."

Usually, during a funeral, people huddle close together, seeking human contact.

"They're the closest-knit family I've ever met," Marie-Pierre says, her voice flat. She's realizing something's not right.

She puts a hand on my forearm, either to get my attention or to get that longed-for human contact that is forever denied us ghosts. "What's going on?"

"I don't know," I reply, my voice serious. "I hope Didier will be able to help us figure it out."

FOUR

DIDIER EMERGES FROM the grave two days later. By then, three new graves have been dug in the southern quadrant of the cemetery and I have a bad feeling in the pit of my stomach that won't go away.

"I can't believe this," are the first words out of his mouth as he crawls out of the grave. "Totally unacceptable." He's a tall man, completely bald, and at least twenty kilos into obese territory. He looks to be in his early sixties.

He catches sight of Marie-Pierre. "Oh, hello Madame Priaux. You're here, too, are you?" Finally free of the dirt, he straightens and stretches his back, then frowns as he realizes this doesn't have its usual effect on his body.

Ghosts don't get back pains—and we can't enjoy a good stretch.

"I'm Robert Villemur," I say, not wanting to wait for the man to ask the questions. "And this is Clothilde. Do you know what's going on? What was your cause of death? That of Marie-Pierre?"

I almost add the three empty graves but decide against it.

Didier gives me a once-over but he doesn't ask any questions. It may appear that if Marie-Pierre is working with me, then I'm okay.

"There's a new virus," he says. "Spreads like wildfire. Attacks the lungs. Especially dangerous to the elderly and those with pre-existing conditions."

He stares daggers at his bulging belly, as if it is the cause of his demise.

"What…" I trail off as I don't even know what to ask him. And even if a killer virus in the world of the living would be a disaster, I'm naturally more turned toward its effect on our ghostly world.

I've talked quite a bit with Marie-Pierre these last couple of days and I cannot figure out what her unfinished business is. If we don't know what the problem is, we can't solve it, and we can't send her off to the other side.

I hold up a hand, palm out. "I want to hear more about this virus, Monsieur, but I have one other pressing question first. Do you happen to know if you have any unfinished business with the living that might be keeping you from moving on?"

"Moving on." Didier turns in a circle to take in our little cemetery. "You mean this isn't the final stop?"

"Next to last," Clothilde says from her perch on a nearby mausoleum. "The one where you can tie up those last loose ends."

Didier nods a greeting to Clothilde. "Mademoiselle. Didn't see you there."

"From what I've understood, Didier," Marie-Pierre says as she pushes her rhinestone glasses up her nose, "ghosts only linger when something is keeping them back. Finding the person who murdered them, speaking to a loved one one last time. Apologizing to estranged family members. Personally, I can't think of anything, but then my mind isn't what it used to be, so maybe I've forgotten?"

"That doesn't seem likely," I hasten to reassure her.

Didier shifts from foot to foot, his forehead creased into a giant frown while he considers the question. "Can't really think of anything." His voice is soft. "Wouldn't mind seeing my family again, but they know I love them. Got along with everyone. And it wasn't a person who killed me, it was this blasted virus."

Could their unfinished business really be with the virus? How is that supposed to work? How can a group of ghosts in a cemetery fight something as intangible as a virus?

I look toward Clothilde but her gaze is turned in the direction of the parking lot.

Two hearses just arrived.

FIVE

"It's the Moulins," Didier says. There's a fatality to his tone that makes me think he's not surprised to see this particular family.

As the two caskets are pushed toward the church, three other cars arrive, with five people in each car. I assume they're the living members of the Moulin family. They vary in both shapes and sizes, ages and color. One of the men in the last car, a man who must be well past fifty, has a dry cough and leans heavily on a man I assume to be his son as they follow the caskets.

"You're not supposed to come out if you're sick!" Didier yells at the man. "Protect the rest of your disease-ridden family, man!"

Didier faces me, fire in his eyes. "What are the rules here? They can't hear me, I suppose? Can I touch? What can I do?"

"They can neither see, hear, or feel you," I say. "And you can't leave the confines of the cemetery. But sometimes their subconscious *can* get our messages. So it's always worth a shot, but it takes patience."

Didier is studying me a lot closer all of a sudden. "Have we met?" he asks, frowning fiercely. "I didn't catch your name."

"Robert Villemur," I reply.

"The cop," Didier says. "I remember when you went missing."

My eyebrows shoot up and if I'd still had a beating heart, it would have sped up considerably. It's the first time another ghost has recognized me, in all my thirty years in this place.

I'm not buried with the rest of my family. I've never had visitors. I don't even have a proper tombstone, just a slight bump in the grass next to Clothilde's grave.

I have no idea if anybody who cares even knows I'm buried here.

I'm about to say as much when my attention is drawn to the two new caskets. "They're not going into the church?"

The procession is almost all the way to the newly dug graves already, the Moulin family trailing behind. The priest, walking ahead of the caskets, and the funeral agents managing the caskets, are all wearing masks and plastic gloves.

"There's less chance of the virus spreading outdoors," Didier says, before running toward the coughing man.

The rest of us follow at a more leisurely pace.

"The entire family has a tendency to attract all types of diseases," Maire-Pierre says in a low voice. "Diabetes, high blood pressure, pneumonia, cancer. You name the disease, one of the Moulins will have it. Every time I went to Didier's office for an appointment I would meet at least one of them."

Didier is speaking directly into the ear of the man with the cough, trying to convince him to stay away from his other family members. He also yells at the whole group to keep their distance.

When the two caskets are lowered into the ground, Didier comes back to join us. "It's Gérard and Claude," he says to Marie-Pierre. "Two elderly brothers," he adds for my benefit. "The fathers or uncles to most of the people here."

We watch in silence as the priest holds his sermon at the graveside instead of inside the church. I'm fascinated to participate in this part of the funeral for the first time since my own demise. Usually, we only get the last words once the casket is in the ground.

I learn something new, too: ghosts wake up when the mass is over. Everybody echoes the priest's "Amen," and the yells start.

"Gérard! Where are you? What is going on?"

"Claude? Where am I? Why is it so dark?"

Clothilde glances up at me and curls her upper lip.

Two more ghosts.

SIX

For two weeks, we continue down the same slippery slope.

Six more funerals, six more ghosts—and fewer and fewer mourners attending the funerals.

We've received the coughing man from the Moulin family, and the overconfident cousin from Marie-Pierre's funeral, the one who insisted on kissing the cheek of the woman who'd spent time taking care of the sick Marie-Pierre.

Marie-Pierre was devastated to discover he'd died—and then proceeded to give the man the talking-to of a lifetime for taking such a big threat so lightly.

For the last funeral, the final journey of one Mathilde Joubert, the thirty-six-year-old cashier at the local Lidl, only her mother shows up to say her goodbyes.

When Mathilde crawls out of the grave four days later, there are twelve ghosts waiting for her.

I've sat down with all our new arrivals over the past weeks, digging into their histories and reasons for becoming ghosts. With the possible exception of a man who hasn't seen his children in over a decade, I find no unfinished business we need to settle, no reason for all of them to linger.

Except the virus.

But what can I possibly do about this thing from the confines of our cemetery? What could I do even *outside* of the cemetery? I don't know how to defeat a virus. I don't know how to bring it to justice.

When we go a week without any new funerals, I tentatively hope we've seen the worst of it. Ten deaths within a month is a very high number for such a small village.

Ten ghosts for ten deaths has never happened—at least not in my thirty years.

Clothilde and I have started taking daily walks around the cemetery, just the two of us, to get away from the others for a while.

We've been used to it being just the two of us for so long, it's hard to adapt to having enough ghosts to make up an entire soccer team. So we take these walks, and pretend we're back to normal for a short hour every day.

"You think the gardener will be back soon?" Clothilde asks as we step through the growing weeds along the west wall.

I run a hand through the pale purple wisteria adorning the cemetery wall, wishing I could still smell their sweet scent. "The lockdown is apparently scheduled to end in two weeks," I say. "I'm guessing our gardener will be back then."

Right now, with nobody doing any kind of upkeep while the spring sun is shining beautifully, our cemetery is looking more and more abandoned by the day.

Or like an overgrown English garden.

I'm starting to think that nature gaining turf might not be such a bad thing.

Apparently, outside, the entire world has shut down in order to stop the virus from spreading. Schools are closed, restaurants are closed, concerts are canceled, people are working from home…. And everyone is sheltering in place, waiting for the plague to pass.

Yet in our cemetery, everything is the same.

Except for the growing weeds—and the ten extra ghosts.

And the lack of visitors.

"We haven't had a single visitor since this all started with Marie-Pierre's funeral," I say. "Do you think that could be what sets them free? They need to say proper goodbyes to the people they left behind?"

Clothilde shrugs. "Except for that one guy, they don't seem to feel too strong a need to say goodbye. And for *all* of them to feel that way?" She trails off and jumps up to walk on the wall. Well, she's walking on air right *next* to the wall—we can't cross the middle of the stone construction.

"I don't like having so many people here," she says as she carefully puts one foot ahead of the other, arms out for balance—as if there's any risk of her falling down.

"I know," I say.

Ironic, really, that we should spend so much time worrying about being all alone and then complain when we finally have company.

"The visitors should come back once the lockdown is over," I say. "Maybe we'll get some answers then."

And in the meantime, we'll try to pretend to be extroverts and enjoy the new company.

SEVEN

MID-MAY, UNDER A beautifully clear and blue sky, with the sun shining down on the living and dead alike, the lockdown is lifted.

Everybody gets visitors on the very first day. Clothilde and I were feeling crowded with ten extra ghosts—now add in hundreds of live visitors.

Clothilde turns into a gloomy teenager and follows some of the louder visitors around, telling them to be quiet and testing their sensibility to ghosts to determine if there is any point in attempting a prank.

I leave her to it.

I decide to join Marie-Pierre at her grave when her daughter comes with a bouquet of orange roses.

"They're from the garden," the middle-aged woman says. "You always seemed to love to come visit when that rose bush was in bloom." She looks to be in her fifties and is wearing a pair of washed-out jeans and a simple black T-shirt. Her hair is short and has dark blue highlights.

Marie-Pierre caresses her daughter's cheek with the backs of her fingers. "I loved to come visit any time." Her hand goes to the blue streaks. "When did you do this?"

The daughter must be sensitive to ghosts because her hand goes to her hair. "I got so bored during the lockdown," she says with a wistful smile. "Figured a little color in my life wouldn't hurt."

Marie-Pierre seems happy.

But she's not fading. Seeing her daughter again and having the chance to say goodbye is clearly not going to be enough for her to move on.

Someone seems to be causing a scene near the parking lot.

At first, I figure it's the live people—they outnumber us at least one to five, after all—but then I realize only the ghosts are reacting. Marie-Pierre is lowering her glasses to look toward the noise, and I see Didier straightening from where he was crouching next to a young girl at his own grave.

It's the beer-bellied cousin.

"What is that idiot Vincent up to now," Marie-Pierre says under her breath as she pushes her glasses back up her nose.

"Looks like he's not happy with his cousin," I say. "The

woman who cared for you before you died?" I think that's her coming through the main gate right now and even though I can't make out the words, the anger and fury in Vincent's voice carries and clashes with such a beautiful sunny day as he hovers over her and yells straight into her face.

I rush to the poor woman's rescue but Clothilde gets there before me.

We might not have physical forms but we remember how things used to work. So when Vincent receives Clothilde's angry eyes right in front of his own face, he takes a step back.

"*What* is your problem?" Clothilde hisses.

The live woman draws a shaky breath and runs a hand down her face but she keeps moving, toward Marie-Pierre's grave if I'm not mistaken.

"What is my problem?" Vincent is not backing down from Clothilde and even goes to far as to try to push her away.

His hands go right through her.

He recovers quickly, though. "My problem is that I'm dead because of that woman. She had the virus and gave it to me and now I'm dead!"

"That's hardly fair, Vincent," Marie-Pierre says. She has joined us by the main gate. There's an entire area that the living are currently avoiding, though none of them will realize it's because there's a fight between ghosts going on.

Marie-Pierre shows she has learned to master the rules of being a ghost as she stands on thin air to get right into her grandson's face. "If she had the virus, it was because she caught it from me. Does this mean you are blaming me for your death?"

"Well…no, of course not," Vincent stammers. "It's not like you gave it to her on purp—"

"Did she go out of her way to give it to you? Cough into your face? Touch your hands?"

I see the moment Vincent thinks he's found a way out. "At your funeral, she—"

"She told you not to get near her," I say. "And yet you insisted on kissing her cheek anyway."

He sputters some more, until he realizes there's now a total of ten ghosts surrounding him, and not a one who seems likely to take his side.

Finally, he mutters, "So you're saying it's *my* fault."

Marie-Pierre tuts at him and pats his cheek. "It's nobody's fault, Vincent. *C'est la vie.*"

I can tell from her expression that Clothilde wants to point out that it's actually death, but luckily, she refrains.

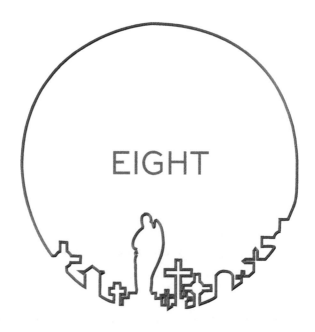

EIGHT

As the cemetery is closed for the night, all the ghosts gather around Marie-Pierre's grave. Being the only one buried in an already existing grave, she's the only of the new arrivals with an actual tombstone, albeit still without her name on it. Some are sitting on the large slab of granite covering the tomb, others are standing on the path. Clothilde is perched on a neighboring headstone.

I'm off to one side, arms crossed and feet wide. I know the stance is a little aggressive but not figuring out what everybody needs is getting on my nonexistent nerves.

"Did everyone get visitors today?" I ask the group, and they nod or reply in the affirmative with expressions ranging from grinning to worried frowns.

"Yet nobody moved on." I tried making time for everyone throughout the day, to listen in on their "conversations" with their loved ones, but still, nothing jumped out as an obvious reason for lingering.

With one notable exception. "Vincent," I say, "I think if you can forgive your cousin for giving you the virus, or accept your part of the responsibility, that might be enough."

After a quick glance at the glaring Marie-Pierre, he mumbles, "There's nothing to forgive. It was nobody's fault."

Right. Now what?

As the last sunlight disappears below the horizon, we sit in silence. I'm all out of ideas and cannot even imagine what living in this cemetery will be like if we're going to be twelve instead of two.

"It's a beautiful night," Marie-Pierre comments. "So odd, that the world keeps turning without us."

"All my patients will have to find a new doctor," Didier says.

"Our kids are going to fight over those houses we own together for decades," Gérard says, and his brother Claude nods.

"My cousin is going to feel guilty about my death forever." Vincent hangs his head.

"So the world keeps turning," Marie-Pierre says. "But not quite the same way."

"A worse way," Vincent says.

"Nonsense." Marie-Pierre's voice has lost its wistfulness. She's dead serious. "It's different, not worse. This virus has changed the world. But change isn't always worse, or better. It's different, and new."

"And it will be different and new without us." Didier's words could be taken as depressing or fatalistic, but his tone is anything but. It sounds like he's made a happy discovery.

Like a responsibility has been lifted.

He throws out his arms to indicate the cemetery around us. "We have a new world to discover. Together."

The mood shift for the entire group comes slowly, but clearly. They're letting go of the anger at having died from some invisible virus they had no control over. They tell each other how happy they are to see that their living relatives seem to be safe and doing well.

And they plan ahead. As a group.

I walk over to stand beside Clothilde. "I think they're planning to stay," I say, low enough that none of the others will overhear.

"Over my dead body." Then Clothilde throws her head back and cackles a loud laugh.

When she calms down, she pats my shoulder. "Don't worry, it won't come to that." She lifts her chin toward the group of ghosts. "They're already leaving."

She's right.

In a large group on the path now, they're slowly becoming transparent. Didier notices first. "What does this mean?"

"You're moving on," I say.

"You're not," Marie-Pierre says.

I shrug. "That's all right. You take care of each other."

Excitement and fear cross their faces as they fade. They grab each other's hands mere seconds before they all disappear.

Silence.

Night has fallen but we can somehow still see each other.

"Wanna go hang out on my grave?" Clothilde says as she jumps down from her perch.

"Always." I follow slowly, reclaiming my cemetery and taking my time to enjoy the return to normal.

And sending up an extra thanks for having my friend here with me.

See? Nobody is alone in death.

FAR FROM HOME

A Ghost Detective Short Story

BOOK 9

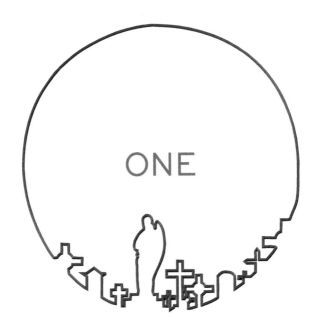

ONE

A CERTAIN PART of me is happy when someone becomes a ghost. It's not something I'm proud of, but I'm self-aware enough to know it's true.

See, when someone becomes a ghost, it's because they have unfinished business, so it's not exactly a good sign. For them. Especially because finishing said business when you're a ghost confined to a cemetery isn't always easy.

I can attest to that myself.

I've been a resident of this cemetery for over thirty years. My unfinished business is atoning for past sins, and I'm atoning by helping others find their peace. In real life I put bad guys in jail.

In the afterlife I teach ghosts about the keys to reach whatever awaits beyond the veil.

Basically, for me, it's a good thing if they're not at peace when they come here. I just need to not focus too hard on the egoistical part of that statement.

Of course, a new ghost also means company.

Now, I'm not exactly alone in this little cemetery. I haunt these hallowed grounds accompanied by my friend Clothilde. She has been here as long as I have and her key to deliverance is as elusive as mine. So despite our apparent differences, we've become close friends.

But years with only one companion can become a little restrictive, no matter how strong the friendship.

So when we hear the screams emanating from the bright white casket as the church doors open after the service, we both perk up.

A new arrival.

Sometimes we hang out by the church when there's a funeral, breathlessly—pun intended, we haven't drawn breath since we died—waiting to see if we'll have company. Other times, like today, we hang out on our own graves.

I blame the weather. Even though we can't feel the temperatures, it's obviously a cool spring morning, with a clear blue sky sporting a single bright white cloud just above the church spire, birds singing in the cypress trees by the main path, and bees buzzing in the wisteria on the north wall.

Lounging seems like a requirement.

So here I am, my ass parked on the small bump in the ground

marking my last resting place, leaning back on my arms, and my legs stretched before me, ankles crossed.

Clothilde is in her usual spot, perching on her gravestone, her hands under her jeans-clad legs, her Converse-covered feet dangling right through the stone. Her youthful face is turned away from me, her expression distant. My theory is that spring is a difficult time for Clothilde because it reminds her of how her life was cut too short—but I'd never discuss such a subject with her. It would earn me an eye roll or a scathing insult. Or possibly both.

Reading into things just isn't Clothilde's style.

Today's funeral procession is a large one. I'm guessing the nice weather had its effect on the number of people who decided to show up, but whoever is screaming his head off in that casket was definitely popular.

Clothilde and I join the mourners as they approach the newly dug grave. Whoever's in there has unfinished business, which means we need to help him finish it. Possibly help him discover what it is. And the people who decided to accompany him to his final resting place may have important information. So we'll eavesdrop on their conversations in the hopes of picking up something that might be useful later.

"He sounds angry, right?" Clothilde casts a glance toward the casket as she studies a woman I assume is the deceased's mother from up close. "Those screams aren't just panic."

We've become experts at interpreting screams. Every ghost screams. Who wouldn't when they wake up in a sealed casket? Only when the ghost accepts he is indeed a ghost will he be released into the cemetery. Some people need only hours, others weeks.

I screamed for five days, which is pretty close to average.

For every single arrival, I pray they'll be quick on the uptake because we have no way of escaping the screams. And listening to someone panic for weeks can be exhausting.

Clothilde is right, though. This guy is more angry than panicked. "Could be a murder victim," I say. "All the more reason to listen in." As I learned as a police officer and have observed as a dead ghost, the chances of his murderer being here are actually quite high.

I let Clothilde focus on the family members up front and wander over to what I assume to be a group of friends toward the back. Two dark-haired men in their late thirties, one blond woman who's obviously just the plus-one of one of the men, and one redhead who's fighting tears.

"I still don't understand why he was home that night," the redhead says, her eyes on the casket. "He was supposed to be in Thailand. They said he used his ticket. How did he even get back?"

The single guy shakes his head. "The police say his business was in trouble. He might have been up to something illegal and using the trip to Thailand as a cover." He sighs. "The fact that he was brutally murdered in what qualified as his office kind of supports their theory."

Definitely a murder case then. Which means our new friend will need for his murderer to get caught in order to find peace.

These cases are always the most difficult ones. Solving a murder while out in the real world is hard enough—doing it from the confines of a cemetery and without the possibility of interacting directly with anyone alive borders on impossible.

We've done it before, though.

"I heard they found proof it wasn't actually Henri on that plane to Thailand," the second man says while trying to free his hand from the death grip his wife has on it. "The images from the airport weren't top quality, but it seems like it was some sort of Henri lookalike."

"So Henri sent someone off as a decoy?" the first man says.

The redhead's lips wobble, but her eyes look angry. "That, or whoever killed Henri planned the whole thing out, and sent a lookalike so nobody would wonder where Henri was until the trail went cold."

Silence settles as the casket is being lowered into the ground.

Although I understand their wish to pay their respects to their friend, I need more information before they're all out of reach. Live people can't actually hear us when we talk, or feel us when we touch them. But there's something. Maybe their subconscious is able to hear what's going on on our side.

I don't know how it works, but I know it does. Sometimes, when we talk to the mourners, they...react to our nudges.

"Who would want to harm your friend?" I ask them. "Could it be linked to this business of his? Did he have any trouble with family members? Will someone benefit from his death?"

Asking a lot of questions in one go like this isn't optimal. The message might get jumbled, and I can end up with nothing. But I'm short on time, and I prefer throwing a wide net in the hopes of catching at least one fish.

"At least dealing with the estate should be easy," the married guy says. "There's nothing but the house, and from what I understand, the bank will take most of that. His brothers should each end up with about five thousand euros when everybody else have grabbed their share."

One motive ruled out.

"I hear Sylvie is furious," the redhead says, keeping her voice low.

All four gazes go to a woman with short dark hair standing alone just behind the family members.

"She'd been fighting with Henri about their business for months. She kept wanting to bring in a new accountant and Henri kept insisting on keeping the one they had because they couldn't afford one who wasn't a friend. Henri told me she was neglecting her parts of the business in favor of criticizing how he managed his."

The married guy sniffs. "Sounds like Sylvie, all right."

I manage to catch Clothilde's eye and point at Sylvie. "She appears to be a prime suspect. See if you can get something out of her?"

"Complicated if she's standing here all by herself," Clothilde yells back. "But all right." She strolls over to the woman and leans in so close their noses almost touch.

The casket is in the ground and the family seems to have said their goodbyes. People are going to start leaving.

"You think the police are going to find whoever killed him?" the single guy says.

"Not a chance." The redhead pulls her black shawl closer around her shoulders. "They have no clue who did it. They'll keep pretending to work the case, but they've clearly been going in circles for weeks already."

As the mourners start moving toward the parking lot, my group follows. I stick close, hoping they'll give me more information, but their conversation just turns to straight out police bashing and I learn nothing useful.

Clothilde catches up to us when we get close to the gate. "There was a guest hiding in one of the cypress trees. I saw one of the branches move and went over to check it out. Guy was getting a cramp." She waggles her eyebrows and her eyes twinkle. "He's definitely related to the dead guy. Looks like a younger, male version of the mourning mother."

Who cares about gossiping friends? A relative hiding in a cypress has a lot more potential.

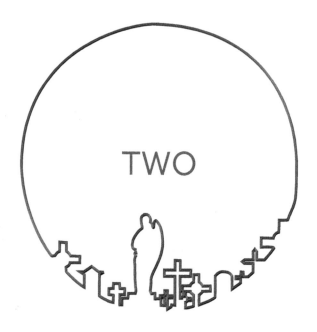

TWO

CLOTHILDE IS RIGHT. The guy climbing out of the cypress tree looks a lot like the grieving mother. There's something in the eyes and the set of his jaw.

"Did you hear talk of any family history?" I ask Clothilde. "Any estranged family member or someone getting criticized for not showing up?"

"No." Clothilde is standing at the foot of the tree, hands on hips, frowning at the man as he jumps down from the lowest branch. "From what I understood, Henri was an only child, so it can't be a brother. Maybe a cousin?"

"There has to be some family feud going on, or he'd participate like everybody else."

"Maybe he's a bastard brother." Clothilde lights up at the idea.

I grunt. "That might work if he looked like the father, not so much when it's the mother." Although I guess it's possible for women to have secret children, it's a lot more difficult for them to keep it a secret from their family. "Also, Henri was apparently thirty-seven, which must be pretty darn close to this guy's age."

"They were twins and the mother decided only to keep one?"

After a quick look to check he's still alone in the cemetery, the man takes off toward the back gate. He doesn't even glance at the fresh grave.

If he'd been here to actually mourn Henri, he would have gone over to pay his respects.

So why the hell is he here?

We have about three minutes before he's out the gate and out of our reach. "How are you related to Henri? Why did you hide in the tree? What are you afraid of?" I bombard him with questions, anything I can think of.

He's not going to answer, of course, unless he's extremely attuned to ghosts. But his subconscious might pick up on something, so I watch his face and his gait, hoping I'll see a tell if I hit on the right question.

I get nothing. His face stays calm and his pace unhurried. When he steps through the back gate, he walks over to an old sedan parked in the shade and drives away.

Clothilde and I are stuck at the gate.

The screams from Henri's grave continue.

THREE

It takes him five days to come to terms with his fate. On the fourth day, the screams become intermittent, during the night he starts knocking on the casket as if testing it for hollow spots, and the next morning, a hand breaks through the newly dug dirt, quickly followed by a head.

Clothilde and I have been waiting at the grave since yesterday. We like to be close whenever someone emerges from their grave. A welcome committee of sorts. Becoming a ghost can be a bit of a shock and I figure seeing a friendly face or two certainly won't do any harm.

"I'm returning to the secret child idea," Clothilde whispers when Henri's head bursts out of the ground.

No kidding. This guy looks nothing like his mother. Or father, for that matter. Both parents were blond, with blue or green eyes. The mother's eyes were set close together, which was what made the man in the tree resemble her so closely. This guy's eyes are brown and wide apart. His nose is kind of big, which was not a trait I saw in any of the other family members.

"Maybe he was adopted?" I whisper back. I stand up and put on a smile. Time for my welcome speech.

When Henri has figured out how to climb out of his grave and he spots us, I nod in greeting. "Hello there, and welcome to our cemetery. My name is Robert, and this here is Clothilde."

Henri frowns as he studies us each in turn, then nods back at me. "I'm Clément."

"Nice to Clément?"

"Yes." He frowns at me as if I'm stupid. "Clément Fontaine. We're all ghosts?"

This is where I usually start my spiel. Explain why he's a ghost, give some pointers on our cemetery, try to figure out what his unfinished business is.

But I'm mute. Can't get a single word out.

My gaze goes to the simple wooden cross that's used to mark the grave until the headstone is ready. It reads Henri Lambert.

Clothilde isn't faring much better. "Uh-oh," she whispers.

"What is wrong with you people—" The man's gaze follows ours. When he sees the name, he stops short. "What the…?"

"You're not Henri Lambert?" I have to ask.

"No." His voice is lighter, as if he's forgotten how to

breathe—which is odd, considering he doesn't need to breathe anymore.

"Well," Clothilde says. "At least that explains why none of the mourners looked anything like you."

I haven't needed to breathe in thirty years, but I'm sucking in air now. "But the guy in the tree did."

Clothilde's eyes widen. "You think that was Henri?"

"I don't know. Makes as much sense as anything else at this point. Does that mean Henri killed Clément? Did he kill someone else so everybody would think he was dead?"

My mind is about to explode. I plomp down on a nearby grave and bury my hands in my hair. How on earth are we going to figure this one out from the confines of the cemetery?

Although Clément initially seemed to have a pretty good grasp of how his ghostly body worked, he's now floating a foot off the ground and his pants have turned into shorts. He's as shocked by these revelations as we are.

"Nobody knows I'm dead? Or where I'm buried?"

"I guess not," I say with a wince. Then I pull myself together. I'm shocked by the revelation, but I'm not the one buried in the wrong grave—actually, I'm the one who doesn't even have a head-stone, but that's a mystery for another day—so I have to be the strong one here. "Do you remember how you died?"

Clément shakes his head.

"What's the last thing you do remember?"

"Waking up inside the casket," Clément whispers.

Clothilde snorts and jumps up to perch on the grave next door. "That part does everyone in, don't worry. Try to focus on something nice from when you were alive. Like having breakfast. Or reading the newspaper. Something positive and focus on the last time you did it."

Feet now close to the ground but still wearing shorts, Clément frowns furiously as he tries to remember.

"I had breakfast at the hotel," he says slowly. "The croissant was stale but the coffee delicious."

"At a hotel?" I ask. "You're not from around here? Just outside Toulouse," I add when he starts looking around, searching for landmarks.

"I'm buried in Toulouse." The poor man looks completely lost. What seems to be a worn teddy bear makes a quick appearance in his right hand. "I'm from Lille," he whispers.

If he's buried on the other side of the country, his family has no chance of figuring out what happened to him.

So I guess we'll have to go at this from the Henri perspective. "It seems likely the reason you were killed was somehow linked to the guy whose name is on your grave." I straighten my spine and take on my police officer voice. Enough panicking, time to start figuring out what happened to this guy. "I'm fairly certain you were either killed by him or in his place. Anything else just doesn't make sense."

"So what do you remember after the stale croissant and good coffee?" Clothilde asks.

Seemingly over the worst of his shock, Clément sits down on the fresh dirt and recounts his last day among the living.

He was in Toulouse on business. He was a contractor and specialized in smart solutions for private homes. Although not for everyone, the people who did want smart houses were ready to pay a lot of money to have the latest technology manage menial tasks for them.

A company in Toulouse promised an interesting solution for making many different appliances work together. If his clients needed four different apps and three different remotes to manage their house, they weren't happy. This guy promised one app could deal with everything.

"This guy wasn't named Henri, by any chance?"

Clément shakes his head. "Bertrand Poulain. But I don't think I ever got so far as to meet with him."

Clothilde swings her legs through the gravestone she's sitting on. "The last hours before death tend to be a little hazy. Where were you meeting him?"

"At what passed for my office while I was in Toulouse," Clément says. "One of those coffee shop/office space things where you can rent a desk by the hour? I usually rent a desk for half a day when I'm traveling, so I'll have a place to work in peace and a place to receive clients and contractors. I don't like always going to them."

"And you remember arriving at the coffee shop?" I ask. I'm not familiar with the concept, but I get the essential idea.

"Yes." Clément nods. Then he frowns. "I do not remember leaving."

Clothilde looks my way and our gazes lock. "He was killed in the coffee shop office thingy?"

"Why would they mistake him for someone else then?" I turn back to Clément. "Do you give your name or show any kind of ID to get a spot?"

"Yes, my name would be in their system."

It's at times like these that I really miss being alive and able to leave the cemetery. What did the police learn at the coffee shop? How many other patrons were there? Did any of them have a connection with Henri or Clément? Was Henri there?

"Henri must have been there, too," I say out loud, as much to myself as to my companions. "If you were killed in that place and they mistook your body for his, he must have at least been scheduled to be there."

"I agree," Clothilde says. "Not that it helps us solve the case or anything. We're not getting anywhere until Henri/Clément here gets some visitors."

She's right, of course. But that doesn't mean we should just sit back and wait.

We have to prepare, so we know exactly what to do depending on who the visitor is.

FOUR

THREE DAYS LATER, Henri's mother comes for a visit. She already came twice while Clément was still in the ground, but she never said anything coherent or interesting and at the time we didn't know what the deal was.

While I'm not at all certain she'll have any useful information for us, we're going to work her as best we can. The number of visitors significantly decreases after a couple of weeks.

Since Clothilde isn't the best with people over fifty, I'm the one who attempts to make contact with the woman as she kneels by what she thinks to be her son's grave. She has brought a single red rose to place on the grave.

"That's a beautiful rose," I tell her. "I'm sure your son would have appreciated it if he'd been the one to be buried here." I'm sitting cross-legged on the grave in front of her, watching for any sign that she hears me. "However, the problem is that the man who was buried here wasn't your son. Which should mean he's still alive and well out there somewhere, while you're mourning him here."

Her face is set in a frown, but it's no different from when she first came here. Of course a mother mourning her son won't be smiling. I'm not sure she's very sensitive to ghosts, which means I won't be getting through to her no matter what I do.

Still, I keep trying. I repeat over and over that her son isn't dead, that she should ask the police to reopen the case because clearly, mistakes were made.

She just kneels there as tears run down her cheeks.

I'm about to give up when Clément rushes up, eyes wide. "A guy came in through the back gate. Clothilde says it's Henri."

I jump up. "The guy in the tree?"

"That's what she said." Clément glances down at the kneeling woman. "She'd recognize her own son, right?"

"I would certainly hope so." God, we'd thought of so many different scenarios, but Henri coming back and running into his mother wasn't one of them. "Why would he come back here and run the risk of getting caught if he was the one to kill you?"

"I didn't recognize him." Clément hasn't been able to remember anything past arriving at the coffee shop, but seeing his murderer's face could have triggered a memory.

Maybe Henri didn't do it?

Leaving the mother behind, I rush after Clément toward the back gate.

The guy who'd been hiding in the tree during the funeral is playing James Bond in between the tombs. Crouching down, popping out his head to scope out the next stretch of gravel path before tiptoeing over to hide behind the next grave.

"I'm less and less convinced this guy is a criminal mastermind," Clothilde says. Arms crossed and lip curled, she'd probably have scared off poor Henri if he'd been able to see her three steps ahead of him.

I have to agree with her assessment. The only reason he hasn't been spotted is that the only live person in the cemetery is his mother, and she's busy crying her eyes out at his grave.

"We have to make sure she sees him," I say. "If the mother sees her son is alive, she'll realize they've buried the wrong person and Clément here can be exhumed and properly identified." At least I hope he will be. Somebody from Lille will have reported him missing by now.

"Clément, you go work on the mother. Tell her to look up from the grave, have a look around the cemetery. Clothilde and I will make sure Henri becomes visible."

Clément takes off with a quick salute and Clothilde and I get to work.

We're aiming for sensory overload. If we can speak loud enough to his subconscious, we might be able to override whatever his conscious brain is trying to think.

"You're not really hidden over there," Clothilde croons into his left ear. "Anybody can see you. You'd be much better off on the other side. Have you seen those houses over there? Lots of windows. I bet there are people looking for you and you're basically in plain sight."

"Your mother clearly misses you," I say into the right ear. "She's over there crying at what she thinks is your grave. Can you see her? Can you see her pain? That's because of you."

And on and on we go. Clothilde playing up his paranoia and me aiming for the heartstrings.

At first, it doesn't seem to work. He keeps moving from grave to grave, staying out of sight from his mother.

But then he throws a glance over his shoulder.

"Ah! Did you see the movement in that window over there?" Clothilde is having way too much fun with this. "I think someone saw you."

Henri steps around the grave he's hiding behind to stay out of sight of the nonexistent persons spying on him from the house. The movement puts him in sight of his mother.

Who unfortunately isn't looking in our direction.

But Henri is looking at her.

"See how sad she is?" I say. "You're the reason she's suffering, why she'll probably never again be truly happy. No parent really survives losing a son, you know."

I just wish I wasn't speaking from experience. After thirty years in this place, we've seen our fair share of grieving parents coming to their children's graves, and it's never a pretty sight. Henri may not be directly responsible for Clément's death, but he is responsible for his mother's pain.

I must be getting through somewhat because Henri has

stopped moving. He's staring at his mother, eyes wide and mouth working soundlessly.

And she still isn't looking up, despite Clément clearly trying his best.

"Oy!" Clothilde screams. "Lady! Over here!"

I jump a foot in the air, and even Henri seems startled. Then even more paranoid, when he can't figure out where the sound came from.

But more importantly, the mother looks up.

She recognizes her son instantly.

"Don't you dare run." Clothilde is practically growling into Henri's ear. "She knows you're alive now. You're not going to add insult to injury and disappear again."

He's on the verge or running anyway. But when his mother's incredulous cry sounds out across the cemetery, he caves.

Gulping loudly, he goes to meet his mother.

FIVE

Henri and his mother meet in the middle of the cemetery. The mother wraps her arms around him and squeezes him so hard he has trouble drawing breath.

Us ghosts settle in on the surrounding graves to watch the show. They don't need any more prodding at the moment.

"Henri, you're alive! How is this possible?" The mother pulls away only far enough to put one hand on her son's cheek. "You were dead. We buried you. How can you be alive?"

"Somebody else was buried in my place, Maman," Henri says. His voice is wobbly with emotion, but I'm not sure which one. "Some other guy was killed in my place. I was supposed to be at that table, because that's always my table, except that day somebody else booked it and I ended up in the corner booth instead."

Tears are streaming down the mother's face as her hand keeps touching her son's face to make sure he's actually there. "But my dear boy, why didn't you tell anybody it wasn't you? What kept you from speaking up? We thought we'd lost you!"

Ah, the beginnings of anger. I estimate Henri has two minutes max before he gets the talking to of a lifetime.

"The killer thought I was at my usual spot, too. He was after me, Maman! I heard him say my name before pulling the trigger. He said something about not knowing when to quit. Someone wants to kill me, Maman. I didn't want them to know they got the wrong guy, so I went out the back door and didn't dare come home."

"That was three weeks ago! Surely you could have found the time to tell your poor mother you were alive since then?"

The mother is no longer holding her son. Her hands are balled into fists at her sides as she glares up at him. "Or do you not care about your family at all? The pain of losing you is just something we should suffer because you're a coward?"

"Ouch," Clothilde says.

Clément sighs. "So it looks like I was killed for being in this guy's place at the wrong time? Great."

Dying for being in the wrong place at the wrong time is never easy to swallow. We've had a couple of these cases over the years, and generally, what they need to move on is to accept their fate in a c'est la vie kind of way. Clément isn't fading, though, despite apparently accepting the truth, so there must be something else he needs.

"I wanted to tell you!" Henri pleads with his mom. "But at first I assumed they would quickly discover I wasn't the guy who got his head blown off, so I decided to take what little extra time was given to me and go into hiding. Once the killer discovered I was alive, he'd come after me again!"

"What about Thailand?" the mother asks.

Henri has the decency to look shamefaced. "I sold it, along with my passport, to a guy evading arrest. I needed the money to save my business!"

The mother seems to decide she's going to let that one slide. She has enough to deal with. She glances at the fresh grave. "There's somebody else buried in there. The poor soul who was shot in your place."

"And I'd greatly appreciate it if you could inform the police of that fact," Clément shouts.

"Maman, somebody wants me dead!"

I'm going to assume Henri is too lost in his own panic to really see the look his mother sends him, or he'd have been running for the hills with his tail between his legs. "Which is why you have to go to the police, Henri! They can protect you. It's their job! Unless you were involved in something illegal? Even then! They don't condone murders, no matter who the victim is!"

"But…"

"Oh my God!" The mother throws her hands in the air and starts pulling her son toward the parking lot. "This is probably why they wanted to kill you, you know. Because that business of yours is on the verge of collapse and instead of admitting defeat, you let the misery drag on forever, just like you did when you were a kid. Sometimes, you just have to admit you failed and try something new!"

Although I'd love to listen in on this conversation for a while longer—this is the best entertainment we've had in years—they are about to pass through the gate and be out of our reach. And I need to make sure one message has come across.

"Please make sure to tell the police about the man who's actually buried here. His name is Clément, and his family doesn't know what happened to him."

Henri is still caught up in his self-pity, but the mother hears me. She looks over her shoulder toward the grave that was meant for her son and frowns. "We're going straight to the police, Henri. So that they can get the guy who wants to kill you, but also so that they can figure out who that poor soul is.

"You didn't only hurt your family with this nonsense, you hurt his too."

She pulls Henri toward his car like he's a screaming toddler, and two minutes later, it's just the three of us left in silence. Hoping the mother will come through on her promise.

SIX

CLÉMENT IS UNDERSTANDABLY nervous as we wait for news. What if Henri convinces his mother that the danger is so great he should just stay in hiding? What if the mother's love for her son, and her fear of losing him again, outweighs her need for setting things right?

After all, they could let Henri stay officially dead and thereby keep him safe.

Which would leave Clément here, without any means of finding justice.

Although Clothilde and I have managed to solve a number of difficult cases over the years, figuring this one out without anyone who actually knew the victim ever showing up would be an impossible mission.

Three weeks after the visit, we're on the verge of giving up, when a team of gravediggers rolls into the parking lot, closely followed by a police car. The gravediggers' van is a fairly usual sight and could simply mean there's going to be a funeral soon, but the police car is not ordinary.

Two officers exit the car, and help a middle-aged, dark-haired woman out from the back seat.

"That's my mom." Clément sounds like he doesn't quite believe his eyes, and he's staying perfectly still where he's sitting on one of the cemetery's oldest tombs, as if worried the illusion will break if he moves.

"Henri's mother won through, then," Clothilde says from her perch on the next grave over. "No doubt about who has the balls in that family. You think Henri is at home, hiding under his bed?"

I chuckle. "My bet is on filing for bankruptcy. That's what the killer wanted, right? So if he officially goes out of business, there should be no more reason to kill him."

There's a chance we'll never know what happened to Henri, and that's just fine with me. He's not the one I'm responsible for—Clément is. Henri has his mom to get his act together and set the police on the tracks of the killer.

I have an hour, max, to help Clément figure out what his unfinished business is.

"Once your casket leaves the cemetery, you'll go with it," I tell him. "You'll be stuck wherever your body is. You need to figure out what your unfinished business is and deal with it. Then it won't matter where your body is, you'll move on to a better place."

Clément is barely listening as he walks pretty much inside one of the police officers holding his mother up, so he can stay close to her.

"If what you need is to find your killer, you'll want to convince your mother to come visit your grave often so she can give you updates."

"I don't care about the killer," Clément says absently. "He wasn't after me, so if he gets caught or not doesn't really change anything for me. I'm dead either way."

Seeing the way he looks at his mother makes it clear just how different Clément and Henri are. One couldn't be bothered to tell his mother he was alive, while the other is clearly worried how his mother will take his passing away. "Maybe what you need is simply to say goodbye properly to your loved ones," I say. "For them to know what happened to you."

Clément's mother has reached the grave, where the grave-diggers are already at work. The two police officers, one looking a little green around the gills from having a ghost inside him for the last five minutes, bring her to a bench farther down the path, so she can watch as they exhume her son.

Once they move away, Clément starts talking to his mother. "I'm so sorry you have to go through this, Maman. I know you always told us we weren't allowed to die before you. But I'm fine now that you'll bring me home to Lille, I promise."

It's difficult to tell if he's getting through. She doesn't show any outward sign of reacting...except she might be a little calmer already.

"You can talk to him, you know," Clothilde says. "Talk to the casket. He can hear you."

Clément turns to glare at Clothilde, apparently annoyed by the interruption.

But then the mother starts talking. "You weren't supposed to go before me, Clément. You knew that." Tears are forming at the corners of her eyes, but she's fighting to keep them from falling. "A mother isn't supposed to bury her son. Or discover he's already been buried in somebody else's grave because the police aren't capable of doing their jobs."

"I'm so sorry, Maman," Clément repeats as he's doing his best to hold his mother's hands where they're folded in her lap.

"I shouldn't have put that kind of pressure on you, though," the mother continues. "Who knows if you'll find peace with the way I've been hounding you all your life to stay alive longer than me. I didn't mean that so literally, son."

"What do you mean?" Clément whispers.

"You and your brothers were so wild when you were younger. Doing crazy thing after crazy thing, giving me heart attacks left and right. Forcing you to worry about me was the only thing that seemed to work to get you to calm down." She sighs. "And here you are, getting killed for working in some other man's spot, through no fault of your own."

Hoping Clément won't mind, I ask the one question I need answered. "How did they know it's Clément in there before exhuming the body?"

I expect another annoyed look from Clément, but he seems too shaken by his mother's words to even notice my interruption.

The mother glances around the cemetery, not really looking at anything. "After that other man showed up alive and kicking, it didn't take the police more than thirty minutes to figure out what happened, you know. One call to that coffee shop and they realized somebody else had paid for his spot that day." A shuddering sigh. "And that someone was reported missing two days after the murder. I guess it's possible it's not you they're going to find in there."

"It's me, Maman," Clément says.

I try to signal to Clothilde. I think Clément is turning transparent. Could this talk with his mother really be everything he needs?

"But I know it's you," the mother says. "I can feel it in my bones. Just like I can feel you're worried about me." She takes a deep breath and straightens her back. "So you listen to me one last time, chéri. Don't you worry about your mother. Your brothers will take care of me. You worry about yourself, and figure out how to find peace, all right? You've deserved it."

He's definitely on his way. He isn't much more than an outline as he clutches his mother's hands. Usually, I say goodbye to ghosts as they move on, but this time I refrain. He doesn't seem to realize what is happening, and I think being with his mother during his last moments is exactly what he needs.

Two minutes later, as the casket is lifted out of the grave, Clément is gone.

"It's a shame," Clothilde says with a lopsided smile. "Now we'll never know what it's like to haunt a plane."

I grin but don't say anything. There's one more thing we need to do here today.

"Your son has found peace," I tell Clément's mother. "You being here and saying the right words helped him move on."

There's no way to know if she heard me, but I'd like to think the nod she gives the casket as it is transported out of the cemetery means she got the message.

And the way her head is held high as she follows in its wake gives me hope she will survive without her son.

Then it's just the two of us left. Clothilde perching on her gravestone and me lounging on my bump on the ground. Waiting for new ghosts to help and working on our own redemption.

SEVERED TIES

A Ghost Detective Short Story

BOOK 10

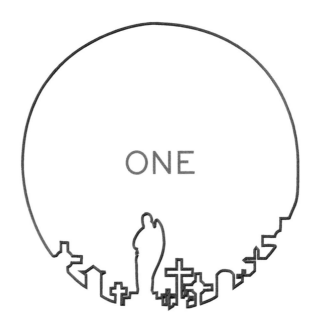

ONE

CHRISTMAS IS A weird time of the year. It can be the most wonderful and heartwarming days of a person's life, just like it can be the absolute worst. There's no in-between. I think the comparison with the perfect days is the reason the bad ones become so bad.

Being ghosts in a cemetery doesn't really change the phenomenon. Except maybe tip the scales away from the cheer and joy.

Now, don't get me wrong. We're not miserable ghosts by any stretch of the imagination. No moaning, very little spooking visitors, no screaming vengeance at the moon. Clothilde tried that last one at one point in the late nineties but couldn't stay serious for long enough to pull it off.

Clothilde and I have celebrated Christmas together more times than either of us did with our respective families when we were alive, and we've developed our own traditions. A couple of times they were adapted because we had a visiting ghost who hadn't resolved their unfinished business yet, but mostly, it's stayed the same through the years.

It starts with the decoration of the church and the manger. We're lucky enough to live in a cemetery belonging to a church where they put the manger outside. If it was on the inside, we could never have seen it. We're stuck on the outside.

There's a sort of shed a little off to the left of the main entrance. I think it might have been intended as a place to park bikes, by someone who didn't realize very few people ride their bike to church. So it has become the setting for a life-sized manger.

The first time they set it up was our second Christmas here. We were both feeling rather blue, missing our families and not yet come to terms with our status as ghosts, and the fuss of setting everything up and working out the kinks turned out to be exactly the kind of distraction we needed.

Joseph and Maria have been here since that first year, obviously, as has the baby Jesus, one sheep, and one of the wise men. I've never been quite clear on which wise man is which—and neither have the people setting it up because the same mannequin never brings the same gift or wears the same clothes two years in a row—but there wasn't enough money to bring them all the first year. The two colleagues showed up three years later, bringing lots of pretty and sparkling gifts.

Better late than never.

I say Jesus has been here from the start, but the one currently waiting to make his grand entrance on Christmas Eve is actually the fifteenth doll playing the part. It's worrisome how popular it is to steal the baby Jesus. I don't think I want to know what happens to them once they leave sacred ground.

The animals have also slowly trickled in over the years. One sheep became five, soon joined by a donkey and a cow. We only have the head of the cow because making the whole thing would be too costly and take up too much space but all the others are the right size and with the correct number of limbs.

Clothilde and I have been known to spend an evening or two inside the manger, sitting next to the wise men or pretending to ride the donkey, feeling a little less lonely for a few blessed hours.

Once the manger is in place, it's the church's turn. Most of the decorations are set up on the inside, so we never see them, but the porch is usually hung with holly and other twigs and greenery, and live lights are set up along the main path from the parking lot to the church entrance for Mass. On Christmas Eve, more than a hundred lights are lit up all across the cemetery.

It's my favorite moment of the year.

Even though our families aren't here and the people setting out the lights never knew us, it makes us feel remembered.

Tonight is December twenty-third and we're spending the evening in the manger. Outside, it's raining and a nasty western wind is starting up, and even though we can't feel the cold or the wind on our ghostly bodies, we can feel the misery. I've opted to sprawl out on the donkey's hay, with my back against the west wall and my legs crossed at my ankles, while Clothilde is perching on the crib. She usually prefers higher ground but the only other option is on the donkey and she doesn't like that for some reason. As usual, her legs swing back and forth, passing through the wood of the crib on every swing.

"I'm telling you, that's Balthazar," Clothilde says, eying the mannequin wearing the blue robes and offering a gilded box to the empty crib where the baby Jesus will lie. The box is empty—we checked—but I *think* it's supposed to contain spices of some sort. Unfortunately, I didn't really pay attention to the details of the story of Jesus' birth while I was alive, and access to research materials is woefully slim in a cemetery.

"You're just saying that because it's the only wise man name you know." I eye the box and wonder if I'd even be able to differentiate one spice from another if I still had taste buds. I know I loved cinnamon and clover—but even the memory of their smell eludes me.

Clothilde shrugs. We share a silence—another thing we've become experts at—while Clothilde frowns out at the dreary night. "I wish we'd get a white Christmas for once. Southern France sucks at helping with the spirit of things."

"The last time we had snow for Christmas around here was in 1962," I say. "I was nine." I sigh happily. "It was the most magical night of my life. I made a snowman! Stole a carrot from Maman for the nose and everything."

Clothilde huffs. "I wasn't even born yet. Why couldn't we be buried in the Massif Central or something? I'm sure those guys have snow every Christmas."

The natural answer to that question is, of course, that you don't choose where you're buried based on where there will be snow for the holidays. Your family chooses for you, so they can come visit. Except in our cases, we never get any visits. Our families either don't care or don't know where we are.

Neither option is very uplifting.

We fall back into silence. I listen to the drip of rain on the manger's tin roof and the wind rustling the branches of the nearby trees. No other sounds come from the village, not even a car. Everybody is sensibly at home, preparing for tomorrow's big feast.

Until a car pulls into the parking lot, the light of its headlights pouring through the main gate, lighting up the nearest gravestones.

I exchange a glance with Clothilde. It must be almost midnight. Who'd come here at this time of night and in such weather?

Clothilde jumps out in the rain to get a look. The rain falls right through her—the reason we prefer to stay out of the rain is because it's such a stark reminder we're no longer corporeal. "It's the hearse. They're bringing someone in."

A funeral the day before Christmas? That's bound to put a damper on the holiday spirit.

Rain be damned, we approach the gate to greet the newcomer. Not a large percentage of dead people become ghosts, so chances are this isn't a new arrival, but we like to accompany the casket through the cemetery anyway. Especially on nights like these.

Two men pull the white casket onto the transportation stretcher and gently roll it toward the church's side entrance. We follow close behind.

"No wreaths," Clothilde comments.

"Maybe they'll come later. They don't always come with the casket."

"*Some* always come with the casket."

I sidestep a puddle even though I can't get my feet wet. Clothilde steps right through it. I like to pretend, she doesn't care.

"The funeral must be tomorrow morning or they wouldn't bring the casket in now," I say. "There's no way they'll be holding the Midnight Mass with a casket up front and center."

Clothilde scoffs. "That sounds like a fun funeral, with the casket surrounded by pretty Christmas decorations and reminders of the party the deceased is missing out on."

It does sound like the perfect way to ruin Christmas for this poor soul's loved ones. For years to come.

One of the men releases the stretcher and goes to unlock the door. "Guess we'll see tomorrow if we have a new ghost," Clothilde says, eying the casket. "Wanna make a bet?"

Ghosts only wake up after the service. Betting on whether or not the dead person has unfinished business and will join us as a ghost is one of Clothilde's favorite pastimes. We have no worldly goods to bet and no possible stakes. Still, it was fun to play for a while. Until I realized Clothilde always won.

"I'm good," I tell her. "Why don't you make your prognostic?"

The two men start pushing the stretcher through the door.

"Nah, I don't think—"

A polite knock sounds from the casket. "Hello?" a gentle male voice says from inside the casket. "Can anybody hear me? I appear to be locked in."

The door closes behind the stretcher and it's just me and a shocked Clothilde in the rain.

Seems like, for once, I should have taken the bet.

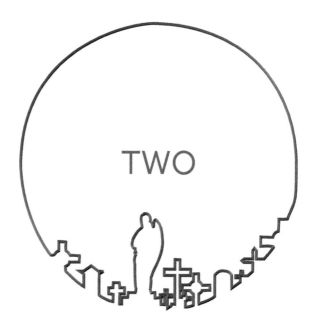

TWO

WHEN THE CASKET exits the church the next day, we're ready for him. Clothilde perches on the staircase railing while I lean against the church wall next to the main entrance. The rain stopped around four in the morning and by the time the sun came up, the sky was a clear blue we don't often see around here in winter, and the temperature must have dropped below zero judging by the state of the rare tufts of grass around some of the less maintained graves. As noon is approaching, a couple of clouds are gathering overhead and more forming in the west. It still qualifies as a beautiful day.

"There are, like, five people max attending the service," Clothilde says. "And I haven't seen any wreaths." Her tone is nonchalant, that of a teenager who doesn't care one way or another. I know it's just posturing, though. Clothilde cares, a lot. And if there's one thing she doesn't like, it's funerals with no loved ones to accompany the deceased to their final resting place.

The fact she probably wasn't accompanied to her own grave *might* have something to do with it.

"We'll see soon enough," I say. They sounded the bells less than five minutes ago, signaling the end of the service. "Do you think he'll come out of the casket straight away?" I ask. I need to distract my friend, but I'm also genuinely curious. "Nobody's ever woken up *before* the service, have they?"

Clothilde shakes her head. "We also usually get screaming and not polite knocking when they wake up."

Yeah, waking up inside a sealed casket? Not fun. Personally, I screamed for days. Don't ask me how it works, but the casket only releases us when we accept we're ghosts. So the duration depends on the person.

The church doors slide open on a creak. I assume a gust of air escapes because a couple of dead leaves blow down the stairs. I can't feel a thing. I straighten and Clothilde jumps down from her perch.

"Hello?" a faint voice says.

Clothilde meets my gaze, baffled. "He's still awake, and still *polite*. How is that even possible?"

I shrug. "I panic when in small spaces. Don't ask me to explain this weird behavior. By all accounts, he should be screaming his head off."

The casket on its stretcher is carried down to the path by six men. One is the priest, and three are cemetery workers we see here regularly. Only two faces are new: a young man in his early twenties with a bright red beanie and a worn bomber jacket, and a woman in her forties with long, salt-and-pepper hair and round, gold-rimmed glasses making her bright blue eyes look perpetually surprised and curious.

"Hello?" the new ghost says again. "Can anybody hear me? I'm not very fond of the dark…."

"Not very fond of—" Clothilde throws her hands in the air. "Nobody is this calm about being dead! That's not human!"

A head pops out of the casket.

Clothilde screams and I skid backward, a hand to my heart even though it hasn't been beating in thirty years.

Without great surprise, Clothilde uses offense as the best defense. "You can't come out of the casket *before* you're buried! You're supposed to crawl out of the ground. Through the dirt. The horror of being buried alive! You can't just *sit* there and say hello like you're a receptionist at a dentist's office."

"Oh." The man turns this way and that, taking in the cemetery and the church. I'd say he's in his mid-fifties, with a huge mop of gray hair and bushy eyebrows. His face is gaunt but there's a kind twist to his mouth and his dark eyes seem to be the keepers of marvelous secrets. I half expect him to invite us into his lap so he can tell us a story.

He's sitting up *through* the casket's lid as if he's in a canoe. Gnarly hands grip the edge—which is a surprise in itself; ghosts usually need some time to learn how to go through some things and on top of others—as he follows the gentle movements of the stretcher toward his final resting place.

"Is this where they're burying me? I must say, it doesn't look so bad." He turns to study me where I'm stumbling along next to the woman with the salt-and-pepper hair, and looks me up and down, taking in my ghostly appearance and the fact I'm walking through gravestones. "Say, Monsieur, would you say this is a decent cemetery to spend eternity in?"

"I, uh…" What am I supposed to answer? "I don't really have much to compare it to." Most people in their thirties don't spend much time in cemeteries—unless they die. In which case you're stuck with the one.

"Yes, of course." He nods to himself before turning to Clothilde.

Clothilde is also keeping pace with the tiny funeral procession, but from a greater distance. I think she's curious—who wouldn't be?—but her expression shows nothing but suspicion. When the man turns toward her, her eyes narrow.

"Delighted to make your acquaintance, Mademoiselle," he says genially. "Théophile Clément, at your service."

Clothilde's expression is nothing short of hilarious. Politeness is not the way to impress girls like her. If she'd still been alive, Clothilde would have been fifty. Clearly, our minds don't age any more than our bodies do once we become ghosts—and doing "old people stuff" is the best way to be ignored by the resident teenager.

Not wanting Clothilde to insult our new friend before he's even out of his casket, I jump in. "That's Clothilde, and I'm Robert. We're the only ghosts in this cemetery at the moment. Tell me, have you been awake for long?"

"Well." Théophile takes another look around, this time taking in the position of the sun and the bare trees of the forest on the north side of the cemetery. "It was Wednesday the last time I went to bed. When I woke up, it was dark and I was in here." He tries to knock on the casket lid, but it turns out to be beyond his capabilities and his hand goes right through. "It's rather difficult to tell time in such places."

"So you couldn't pop your head out until just now?" Clothilde asks. Curiosity is getting the better of her, I'm glad to see.

"I can't say that I tried." Théophile moves his hands through the lid, through the side of the casket, holding on to the rim. "I did an awful lot of knocking but I'm beginning to see this doesn't mean much." He tries knocking from the inside. His hand goes straight though. "Huh. It may appear the casket has only recently opened."

Even with years of practice, Clothilde and I can't knock on anything either. We can make it look like we're knocking, but there is never any sound, be it for the dead or the living. The only time a ghost can make a sound—and it's only audible to other ghosts—is when they're stuck inside the casket. I guess even Théophile had to follow that rule.

The stretcher comes to a stop in front of a newly dug grave. The gravediggers came two days ago, so we knew there would be a burial soon, but we weren't expecting it to happen on Christmas Eve. The three cemetery workers help set up the casket, then leave. The priest stands in his usual spot at the head of the grave, while the woman and young man stand at the foot. Given the distance they keep between them, I assume they're not very close.

Théophile observes all this from his perch in the casket. When the priest starts talking, he leans toward me and whispers, "Do you think I should come out now?"

I hold back my laugh. "You might as well. I've never seen anyone halfway out of their casket when it was covered in dirt before. It might not be the best first experience as a ghost."

"Quite." With great care, he stands up, to display he's wearing a classy but worn two-piece suit, the first two buttons of his white shirt open. He hesitates before stepping out, testing the solidity of the casket.

"You can't affect the physical world anymore, old man," Clothilde says. She's found a perching spot on the Gerard family grave in the neighboring plot. "Nor can it affect you. You can walk on air if you want."

Eying the gap between his casket and the solid earth, Théophile doesn't seem convinced. He very carefully takes a long step, going over the side of his casket instead of simply passing through, and finds himself two steps away from the priest—who seems to be doing his usual spiel for the people he knows nothing about.

"Your family couldn't tell the priest anything about you to make this more personal?" I ask.

"My family?" Théophile is brushing down his suit, convincingly enough that ghostly dust particles fall from his trousers.

I point to the woman and young man at the foot of the grave, both staring intently at the casket. No tears, but that's fairly common, all things considered. Not everybody likes to let out all their emotions when out in public.

Théophile's bushy eyebrows draw together. "I've never seen these people before in my life. Why would you make such an assumption?"

THREE

THERE'S NOTHING LIKE a good mystery to get Clothilde engaged. The minute Théophile tells us he doesn't know his two mourners, she jumps down from her perch and approaches the pair.

She starts with the young man in the red beanie. He stands half a head taller than Clothilde, his hands deep in the pockets of his bomber jacket. Tufts of dirty blond hair curl around the beanie in the back and his deep-set brown eyes stay fixated on Théophile's casket. I don't think he's listening to a word the priest says but I'm willing to bet he's taken note of every single movement the long-haired lady to his left makes.

There's a tension between the two, like either could explode into action at the slightest provocation. I first thought they were members of the same family who had some history.

"I don't think he's had a decent shower in a while," Clothilde comments. "We should probably be glad we don't have a sense of smell, judging by the layer of dirt and grease on his neck."

Beanie-boy must be more sensitive to ghostly activity than most. He lifts a hand to scrub at his neck while he shifts his weight to the other foot.

"Bad teeth, skin that hasn't seen sunblock in years but lots of sun, all of his clothing has seen better days." Clothilde meets my gaze. "I think he might be homeless."

She moves over to the lady. "Doesn't bother coloring her hair to hide the gray. The dress and coat are understated but clean and probably expensive. Those glasses are *gleaming*. It's not possible to have glasses made of actual gold, is it?"

Instead of joining in on the research, Théophile is exploring his new home. Reading the inscriptions on the nearest graves, poking at the plastic flowers on the Gerard plot, gazing beyond the cemetery walls in search of who knows what. When Clothilde mentions golden glasses, he snaps to attention. "Gold is far too heavy for such use. It would be horribly heavy on nose and ears alike."

"Good to know," Clothilde grumbles. Eyes narrowed, she brings her hands to her hips. "If you don't know these two, you might want to help investigate before they leave. Chances are, they're your ticket out of here."

"Ticket out?" Théophile's head whips from one side to the other. Is he looking for a train?

"Only people with unfinished business linger as ghosts," I tell him. With his odd arrival, I haven't even gotten around to doing my usual spiel. "Clothilde and I usually help. Either by figuring out what the unfinished business is, or by finishing it."

"Unfinished business." He says it as if he's trying on the words to see how they taste. "Hah! Hardly surprising I'm there, then. I take it you two would also need decades to tie up everything?"

No, we're still here because we'd need to leave the cemetery to finish our business. Oddly enough, the people who killed us have never come to visit.

Clothilde sneers at Théophile but luckily keeps her thoughts to herself.

"You have a lot of unfinished business, I take it?" I step aside to let the priest access the lift that will lower the casket into the hole without stepping through me. He wouldn't notice—we've met him often enough to know he has no sensibility to ghosts whatsoever—but I hate it.

Théophile goes down on all fours to study the mechanism of the lift. He still hasn't spared his mourners a single look. "I make it a point of honor never to finish anything," he says. "Never saw the point in following other people's orders or bending to their wishes. When I'm done with something, I don't linger. Take high school, for example." He jumps back up and addresses Clothilde directly, for some reason—does he assume she should still be in high school? This won't end well. "Why should I learn by heart the years of such and such battle a random historian has decided were more important than other dates? Why should *they* decide the information to be stored in my brain? I listened to the parts

I found interesting and left to do more interesting things when the testing started."

I groan inwardly. I *really* hope this guy will figure out his unfinished business quickly, because I do not want to spend years and years with him here. Clothilde and I get on each other's nerves sometimes, sure, and bored out of our minds quite often. But we're also best friends and we have a routine. I don't want Théophile to mess that up.

So when Clothilde's temper predictably flares and she stalks away from the two mourners to follow up on Théophile's comments, I take her place. Logically, the answer to our prayers should be with these two. If I could only get them to talk.

Before I can even decide on a line of attack, the woman with the golden glasses turns slightly and gives the young man a once-over. Although the two have clearly been acutely aware of each other throughout the ceremony, this is the first time either has looked at the other.

The man in the red beanie's eyes twitch in her direction but turn back to the lowering casket before their reach their destination.

"She looks like a nice lady," I say to him. "It might be a good idea to talk to her. Figure out what her link to Théophile is."

Live people can't hear us, but the ones who are sensitive to otherworldly activities can somehow absorb what we say to them anyway. I think their subconscious can hear us and brings our words up as ideas to their own minds. Unfortunately, it's not an exact science, but we make do. It's the only way we have of solving dead people's mysteries around here.

The young man's sensitivity is confirmed when he turns to

face the woman. "I'm Xavier," he says in a rough voice. "You knew him?" He nods toward the grave.

The casket is at the bottom and the priest has thrown in his handful of dirt. It seems neither of the mourners have the intention of doing the same and the priest is awkwardly rounding things up so he can leave and get ready for the Midnight Mass. Clothilde is listening to Théophile talk and the way her eyebrows are reaching for the sky is not promising.

The woman's face flickers with what I think is disappointment. "I'm Mathilda," she says and holds out a hand. "And yes, I had the misfortune of knowing Théophile."

Xavier lets out something between a huff and a sigh as he reluctantly shakes her hand after wiping it off on his pants. "I take it I'm not the only one he disappointed in life?"

Clothilde comes stomping to join us, while Théophile seems to be aiming for the nativity scene. The spring in his step is nothing short of joyous. Is it possible to be happy to be dead?

"The guy takes *pride* in disappointing people," she almost growls. "If anyone ever shows the slightest indication of expecting anything from him, he's out. Nobody but Théophile dictates what Théophile does."

I acknowledge what she says with a nod but don't make a reply. I want to hear what Mathilda has to say to Xavier.

"Théophile leaves a *long* trail of disappointed people behind him." There's compassion for the young man in her tone but also a hardness that I'm guessing is especially fitting when talking about our newest ghost. "You shouldn't feel bad about it; it has nothing to do with you personally."

Xavier doesn't look like he believes her, but he keeps silent and burrows deeper into the collar of his jacket. More clouds have blown in during the burial and the lack of sun is probably felt keenly by those who still have corporeal bodies.

"Besides," Mathilda continues, "I'm guessing you're here because you got something from his estate? Nobody else would even know about the funeral."

I'm starting to understand the lack of wreaths and mourners.

Xavier nods. "I've apparently inherited a house." He doesn't seem to quite believe his own words. "Nothing is done according to the current norms because he didn't believe in following rules, but it's still a house. A nice one." His voice cracks on the last words.

"Indeed it is." Mathilda reaches out to pull on Xavier's elbow and the pair walks slowly toward the parking lot. Neither spares as much as a glance at the grave. Clothilde and I trail behind, listening in. "If you got the house, I assume it's because of the law and not something Théophile did?"

A curt nod.

Mathilda pushes her glasses up her nose. "Me, I officially got the half of my business that Théophile still owned. I've managed everything for ten years and he never helped or bothered me, so it won't actually change much. But it's nice to know it's all officially mine."

"We can't let them leave without figuring out what that jerk's unfinished business is," Clothilde says as we approach the gate. Ghosts can't go past that barrier.

"It seems unfinished business is what he does," I reply. "But if it doesn't bother *him*, why would it be keeping him here? There has to be something—hopefully *one* thing—that's unfinished even in his mind."

Two steps from the gate, the young Xavier stops. His gaze is distant and his breath is short. "He's the reason my life is so miserable," he says to his feet. "It's because of him my mom overworked herself so much she didn't realize she had cancer before it was too late. He starts something, gets everybody around him excited to go with him, then drops everything and leaves. At the worst possible time." His anger is taking over, his voice rising and his posture becoming less cowed.

Mathilda nods in understanding and patiently waits for the rest.

"He left two days after I was born," Xavier spits out. "When the hospital staff told him it was his job to do the paperwork to officially name me. Add in my mom expecting him to keep their business afloat for a month and he was gone.

"The jerk was my dad."

FOUR

WE WATCH AS the taillights of Mathilda's car disappear down the road. Xavier was on foot but accepted her offer of a ride to his new home. According to the clock on the church it's mid-afternoon, but it's almost dark already. There's not a speck of blue sky in sight, only heavy, dark clouds. It looks like we're getting a wet and depressing Christmas.

In the company of the most selfish ghost I've ever encountered.

"Having a kid should be important to anyone, right?" Clothilde says. "Even self-centered liars?"

I look toward the church and spot Théophile in the manger, apparently studying the craftsmanship of the cow. "I certainly hope so," I reply on a sigh. "At least it gives us an angle of attack. Except, if his business *is* with his son, I have no idea how we're going to resolve it. I doubt that man is ever coming back here."

Her jaw jutting out with hardened resolve, Clothilde marches toward Théophile like a general going to war. "The issue will be resolved in *his* head. And we're going to figure out how. I'm *not* spending eternity with that loser."

When we reach him, Théophile is riding the donkey, a joyful smile on his face. "It's a shame I can't feel the fur. It looks wonderfully soft."

"You lied to us." Clothilde crosses her arms and widens her stance. If she hadn't been wearing her usual ankle-length jeans and flowing white blouse, she'd look downright intimidating. "You said you didn't know either of your mourners."

By the way his nose tips up and his hands smooth down his vest, I can tell he's going to deny it. Which I don't have the patience for today, so I speak before he can. "The woman was a business associate of yours. It's kind of hard to forget someone you work closely with."

Théophile sniffs. He seems to be about to deny everything, gets a look at Clothilde's furious face, and deflates. "Fine. I knew Mathilda. But I don't see why she'd show up to my funeral. There was no love lost between us. The young man, I've never seen before, though."

"You left him and his mother when he was two days old," I say. "I suppose it's reasonable to assume he's changed since then. Especially since he appears to have been homeless for some time."

That does the trick. Théophile forgets he was sitting on the donkey and is suddenly standing a foot off the ground, halfway through the stuffed animal. He's been quite adept at being a ghost this far, but everyone has their limits.

"That was David?" he asks. His voice is almost uncertain.

"Oh, God, you have even more kids you've run out on?" Clothilde throws her hands in the air and pretends to choke Théophile from afar.

Théophile straightens, and when he realizes he's floating mid-air, drops to the ground. His nose is in the air again. "I have not 'run out on' more than one boy, I assure you. Just the one, about twenty years ago. And his name was David."

"Except you refused to do the paperwork to name him," I say. "And I'm guessing the mom decided *she* wanted to decide the name, since she was the one who had to do everything after you left. His name is Xavier."

"Xavier! But that's— Oh. Well, then." He crosses his arms only to uncross them immediately.

"Would we be right to assume your unfinished business is with your son?" I ask.

"Why would it be about him? I've always made a point of never finishing anything."

"Yes, so we've understood." I glance at the mannequins of Mary and Joseph, already set up so they hover over the empty crib where Jesus will appear tonight. Without the baby, they look kind of sad, like they're happy about a pile of hay while ignoring everybody else around them. Once the baby is in place, though, they'll be equal parts happy and worried parents. Like I imagine most parents feel when they look down on their newborn for the first time.

"Still. Leaving your son behind can't sit entirely right, even with someone used to disappointing everyone around him?"

Théophile huffs. "I don't understand why he was here at all."

"Clearly, the mother did *her* work well, and listed you as the father. The boy just inherited your house, and probably most of your belongings."

The shock of this news is so strong that Théophile's ghostly form flickers. I have a second to hope it means he's moving on, but then he comes back.

Clothilde cackles. "Shocked the state helps you take care of your kid, Théophile? It's very hard to leave your children with nothing in France. And if you don't have a will, they get everything. A case where doing nothing actually is doing something."

That shuts him up. I'm not sure if he needs time to reflect on his life and his choices or if he's avoiding us, but he spends the rest of the afternoon walking the cemetery, discovering his limitations as a ghost. Clothilde and I stay in the manger, chatting about the wise men and their gifts. Maybe we could drop a hint with one of the ladies who set it up for them to properly label the gifts? Twenty years of asking ourselves the same questions get a bit tedious.

When the bells strike nine thirty, people start filing in. Some come by car, quite a few on foot. Most families will start their Christmas feast once they get home, but the ones with very young children have probably already dug into the foie gras. I remember the taste well enough to know I miss it.

We stay in the manger, Clothilde perched on the donkey and me sitting on the floor next to Joseph. This way, when the churchgoers come to check out the nativity scene, it almost feels like they're talking to and seeing us.

Every year, I study every single person passing through the church doors. I know we're not far from the village where I grew up and where part of my family presumably still lives, and I cling to the faint possibility they would come here for Midnight Mass one year. If they do, I don't want to miss it.

This is probably why my first reaction to seeing Xavier and Mathilda show up again is jealousy.

Théophile spent his entire life running from everything—and yet they come back for him.

"Théophile!" I yell into the night. "You have visitors!" An old couple by the stairs startle, and after a shared look, hurry inside the church.

Théophile appears and when he sees his son, goes straight to him. The pair has stopped some distance off, apparently arguing whether or not to attend Mass. Although I frankly don't want to, I saunter over to join them. This *is* our best chance at getting rid of Théophile.

"We've already listened to the priest's yapping once today," Xavier says on a sigh. "Isn't that enough?"

"It's Christmas and you're going home to a feast of buttered pasta for one," Mathilda says with a kind smile. "You can afford to listen to the words of a kind man for an hour or two."

"There's a box of foie gras somewhere in the basement, if you can find it," Théophile says to his son. His voice is distant and the way he's looking at Xavier is very intense. I think he might be trying to see himself in the young man.

"Maybe I'll have a look around in the basement," Xavier says. "See if the old man had any treats hidden away."

Théophile whips around to stare at me.

"Your son is sensitive to ghosts," I tell him. "If you have something to say to him, he might even hear it." As if the man is ready for something as decent as an apology.

"Hey, look," Mathilda says, and points to the sky. "I think it's snowing."

At first I think she's simply trying to get Xavier to think of something else, until a snowflake lands on the young man's nose and promptly melts.

Clothilde appears at my side, her face even more youthful than usual. "It's snowing? For Christmas? Really?"

I can't help but laugh. "Looks like it. Go enjoy your first white Christmas, Clothilde."

On a happy laugh, Clothilde does just that.

Xavier seems equally happy. He tips his head to the sky and closes his eyes, letting the snow fall on his face. "And I'll have a warm bed and a roof over my head tonight," he whispers.

Théophile is the only one in the group who doesn't care about the snow. He's so close to his son's face, it borders on creepy. It's a good thing only us ghosts can see him. "That's not right," he says. "How can a son of mine fall so low he doesn't even have a roof over his head?"

"Maybe he didn't inherit your lack of empathy and sense of community," I say.

Théophile falls silent but doesn't stop his fierce scrutiny of his son. Around us, people are exclaiming about the snow, some happy, some worried about getting home after Mass.

"I didn't know how to be a father," Théophile says. His eyes are still on his son, but I think he's talking to me. "He was better off without me. I would have messed him up, like I do everything. It's no great issue when you mess up a business deal or a friendship. But a fragile, little life? I panicked." He reaches out to touch his son's cheek, but lacking practice, he goes right through. "I did what I thought was best for you, Dav—Xavier. Really."

The young man definitely hears his father. He turns to gaze toward the newly dug grave across the cemetery. "I guess I should thank my father for the house," he says. "He hasn't done anything for me while he was alive, but at least dead, thanks to him, I'll be warm tonight."

Mathilda sighs and gives him a hug. "If I needed proof you're his son, that kind of whacked-out logic will do it. But yes, let's look at the positive side. You have a warm place to sleep tonight, and every other night this winter, and we get snow for Christmas!"

The pair walk into the church and soon, the doors shut behind the last of the revelers. Outside, in the snow but leaving no footprints, stand three ghosts. And let's not forget the mannequins of the nativity scene.

"Seems you managed to help your son, after all," I say to Théophile, who appears to be frozen in place as he stares at the spot where his son disappeared into the church. "Better late than never?"

His confused eyes meet mine. "I helped him?" There's definitely hope in his tone.

"I'd say so. Giving a home to a homeless person definitely qualifies as helping."

"Huh." His eyes go back to the church doors and as a huge smile grows on his face, his body becomes more and more transparent.

I open my mouth to tell him goodbye, or to point out he's finished his business, but in the end I stay silent. I don't want to interrupt the obvious happiness he's feeling. I hope he gets to take it with him wherever he's going next. Despite having been a rather despicable human being, he must also have been very lonely. Finishing off knowing he helped his son feels right.

Five minutes later, an excited Clothilde comes back. "Where'd the jerk go?"

"He moved on."

"Really? That was quick." There's a slight hint of envy in her tone, but I know it won't linger. We're used to being just the two of us and can take years more while we wait our turn.

I'm just glad we don't have to wait with Théophile.

One of the church ladies slips out the side door with a bundle in her arms.

"Ah, here comes the baby Jesus."

So we hold up our own Christmas tradition. We sit with Mary and Joseph as their baby is "born" and watch our cemetery being quietly covered in a blanket of snow with the congregation singing Christmas carols inside the church.

"I've always wanted a white Christmas," Clothilde says happily as she gives the Jesus doll a pat.

See? No need for fancy gifts to have a perfect Christmas.

Also by R.W. Wallace

Mystery

Ghost Detective Novels
Beyond the Grave
Unveiling the Past
Beneath the Surface
Piercing the Veil

Ghost Detective Shorts
Just Desserts
Lost Friends
Family Bonds
Common Ground
Till Death
Family History
Heritage
New Beginnings
Far From Home
Severed Ties
Eternal Bond
Harsh Expectations
Dull Expectations

Ghost Detective Collections
Unfinished Business, Volume 1
Unfinished Business, Volume 2

The Tolosa Mystery Series
The Red Brick Haze
The Red Brick Cellars
The Red Brick Basilica

SHORT STORY COLLECTIONS
Deep Dark Secrets
A Thief in the Night

ROMANCE

FRENCH OFFICE ROMANCE SERIES
Flirting in Plain Sight
Hiding in Plain Sight

STANDALONE NOVELS
Love at First Flight

HOLIDAY STORIES

COLLECTIONS
Heartwarming Holiday Tales

SHORT STORIES
The Case of the Disappearing Gingerbread City
Crooks and Nannies

YOUNG ADULT SHORT STORY COLLECTIONS
Tales From the Trenches

Find all R.W. Wallace's books:

rwwallace.com/allbooks

ABOUT THE AUTHOR

R.W. WALLACE WRITES in most genres, though she tends to end up in mystery more often than not. Dead bodies keep popping up all over the place whenever she sits down in front of her keyboard.

The stories mostly take place in Norway or France; the country she was born in and the one that has been her home for two decades. Don't ask her why she writes in English—she won't have a sensible answer for you.

Her Ghost Detective short story series appears in *Pulphouse Magazine*, starting in issue #9.

You can find all her books, long and short, all genres, on rwwallace.com.

Milton Keynes UK
Ingram Content Group UK Ltd.
UKHW021541070524
442346UK00039B/333

9 782493 670168